SHARON McCONE MYSTERIES
BY MARCIA MULLER

MARCIA MULLER

THE TREE OF DEATH

THE MYSTERIOUS PRESS

Published by Warner Books

A Time Warner Company

MYSTERIOUS PRESS EDITION EDITION

Copyright © 1983 by Marcia Muller
All rights reserved.

Cover design by Jackie Merri Meyer
Cover illustration by Phil Singer

This Mysterious Press edition is published by arrangement with the author.

The Mysterious Press name and logo are registered trademarks of Warner Books, Inc.

 Mysterious Press books are published by
Warner Books, Inc.
1271 Avenue of the Americas
New York, NY 10020

W A Time Warner Company

Printed in the United States of America

First Mysterious Press Printing: April, 1996

10 9 8 7 6 5 4 3 2 1

For Sam

THE TREE OF DEATH

ONE

I STARED IN DISBELIEF AT THE TICKET UNDER THE WIPER OF MY VW Rabbit, then snatched it up. Code 27368. What the devil was 27368? I turned the ticket over and scanned the list of things deemed offensive to the city of Santa Barbara. Failure to register vehicle.

"Maldito!" I hurried around the back of the little yellow car and looked at the license plate. Sure enough, the sticker showed re-registration had been due in April. Today was May second.

I glared at the plate, then tore the ticket into two pieces and dropped them on the ground. Normally I'm a very law-abiding person, but this was too much.

"They could give you a few days' grace," I muttered as I walked toward the museum. It was, of course, because of the museum that I'd forgotten to send in my registration fee. The form was sitting on my desk at home, but what with moving and unpacking the exhibits, the upcoming press preview and the opening, I hadn't been home long enough to write the check.

Still, it was worth it, I thought, feeling a rush of pride as I approached the nineteenth-century adobe that now housed the Museum of Mexican Arts. A month ago we'd been in a storefront in the seediest part of the city; now we were ensconced in a historic building in Pueblo Viejo, Santa Barbara's Old Town. The museum was young as museums went—five years old—and much too poor to afford such elegant quarters, but the adobe had been an unexpected bequest from a deceased board member.

I stopped in the archway leading to the central courtyard and admired the blue-tiled fountain. It had been plugged up when we moved in, but I'd found a plumber who was willing to donate his services, and now the water flowed merrily, the late morning sun sparkling on it. The court-yards and little gardens that surrounded the building were full of flowers—hydrangeas, azaleas, poinsettias—by virtue of our director's knowledge of horticulture.

One of his few virtues, I reminded myself as I turned and spotted him standing inside the entrance to the galleries. Frank De Palma was a fat, curly-headed man who, in spite of his custom-tailored suits, always managed to look as if he had just been shopping at the Salvation Army. He stood admiring the colonial gallery in much the same way I'd admired the fountain, hands clasped behind him. There the resemblance stopped, fortunately. Frank's tie was askew, his shirt bulged over his enormous stomach, and one of its buttons was undone, exposing a roll of hairy flab. I shuddered and looked away.

It wasn't Frank's sloppiness that bothered me, though.

That I could forgive in anyone, provided he was a competent administrator. But Frank was lackadaisical at best, and since our move he'd been too excited to do a lick of work. We couldn't even get him to sit down at his desk; he spent most of his time wandering as he was now or regaling his entourage—a group of men I privately referred to as the Mexican Mafia—with tales of his fund-raising prowess. Well, Frank *was* good at getting people to cough up money, which was why our board of directors put up with him.

When I turned around again, he was gone. I crossed to the door and let myself into the colonial gallery. The centuries-old religious figures from the era when Mexico was ruled by Spain looked especially serene in their new display cases, protected at last from curious hands and the elements. My arrangement of three crucifixes really worked, in defiance of Frank's contention that it was just too much gore in one place. I'd overruled him on that one—after all, I was curator here—and I was glad I had. Nodding familiarly at a Virgin Mary, I went on through the galleries, making a final check on placement before I returned to my desk.

In the folk art gallery on the far side of the courtyard, I came upon a stocky young man with an unruly mop of black hair. Jesus Herrera, a local artist and creator of fantastical papier-mâché animals. He stood almost in an attitude of prayer, gazing up at one of his brilliantly colored dragons, which hung from the ceiling.

"Hi, Jesse." I addressed him with the nickname he preferred to the biblical appellation.

Jesse turned, his shoe-button eyes shining. "Elena Oliverez! It's wonderful how you've arranged them!" He gestured at the dragon and then at the iguana with butterfly wings. "My little *camaleones* have never looked better."

Camaleón—chameleon—was Jesse's name for his colorful creations. He claimed the exotic animals changed according to their setting, the angle at which they were viewed, and, of course, the eye of the beholder. I had to agree with him.

"I'm glad it pleases you. The *camaleones* should get plenty of attention from the press if the preview comes off as planned."

"Why shouldn't it?"

I shrugged. "It should. The exhibits are in place. The food's been ordered. The volunteers have been lined up to serve. The press kits are assembled."

"So what could go wrong?"

"I don't know, but if something can, it will."

Jesse grinned wickedly. "Nonsense. The only thing you have to worry about is getting old Frank here on time, without egg all over his tie."

"Don't worry about Don Francisco; worry about me. I'm exhausted, but I can't sleep. My head aches. I went to the drugstore for aspirin a few minutes ago and found a ticket on my car. There's a sinkful of dirty dishes at home. If I don't do my laundry tonight, I won't have anything to wear to the preview."

"Poor Elena. You work too hard."

"Tell that to the boss."

"No, thanks. The only member of that family I'm interested in talking to is Maria."

Maria was Frank's twenty-year-old niece and the museum secretary. "You're still hung up on her, eh?"

"Hung up?" Jesse assumed a dignified pose. "We are in love."

"I thought Frank told you you couldn't be."

"Not exactly. He said that if we were I'd better forget about exhibiting here."

"That must have been a heated exchange."

"Sure was." Jesse's shoe-button eyes became hard and flat-looking. "I offered to break his fat neck."

His cold anger made me uneasy. Jesse, like so many of us, was an emotional person, subject to instanteous mood shifts. Such shifts could be dangerous.

Apparently he saw the concern on my face because he smiled reassuringly. "Oh, don't worry, Elena. Tío Taco doesn't bother me. But is so sad—Maria De La Cruz, the fairest girl ever to travel north from Mazatlán, in bondage to that fat slug." Quickly he had slipped into the cadence of his native tongue, rhythms I heard in my own speech, in the speech of all of us who had grown up in Spanish-speaking homes.

I smiled too. "I don't think Frank exactly keeps her chained up."

"Ah, they are chains you cannot see. During the day she is handcuffed to that typewriter, for a peon's wages, which she must return to him for room and board. And on the weekends he forces her to clean the office. But the evenings are worst of all because then she must look after his five gordicitos."

I laughed. "Little fatties" did indeed describe the De Palma children. Maria's lot in life was not easy. "And then there's Robert."

Jesse clapped a hand to his forehead. "You had to mention him. Roberto De Palma. Fat, forty-five, and dull of intellect. Personally, I think he's genetically unsound. Does Tío Taco really think he can marry Maria off to his brother?"

"Well, he's not a relation. Maria's Frank's niece on his wife's side."

"But—Robert?"

"Well, you do have a point."

We fell silent. The camaleón above our heads stirred faintly in the breeze from the ventilation system.

"Are you here to see Maria?" I asked.

Jesse shook his head. "We decided to cool it. Tío Taco's always lurking in corners these days."

As if on cue, Frank entered the gallery with Antonio Ibarra in tow. Tony was one of the entourage, a scrawny, pale-skinned man who had recently emigrated from Bogotá, Colombia, with his teenaged bride. Officially his position at the museum was education director—a farce, since he was not too bright and had at best an indifferent command of the English language.

Tony's real function was as Frank's whipping boy. Our director ordered him around, sent him on unimportant errands, and referred to him in his hearing as "my stupid Colombian." Tony, on the other hand, acted as if he thought Frank's abusive behavior merely amusing and had adopted toward the rest of us an attitude of hauteur that bordered on the ridiculous. Fortunately, one of the volunteers had handled the educational materials before Tony's arrival and had merely continued to do so after he was hired.

Frank nodded distantly to me, glared at Jesse, and continued through the gallery. Tony smirked at us both and followed with his peculiar, slouching gait. I waited until they were out of hearing, then said, "Why does the term 'lounge lizard' come to mind?"

"Tony, you mean?"

"Yes."

"Because he looks like a lizard and he's always lounging around."

"Trust you to explain it." I glanced after the two men. "I'd better get back to my desk, see what disaster has befallen us in my absence."

"Sure. Say hi to Maria for me." Jesse turned back to the *camaleón*, once again assuming a supplicant's stance.

Actually, we didn't need a disaster to befall us; my desk was one. The in-box was piled perilously high. Orange press kits were stacked on one corner, and some had toppled over onto the Peruvian rug. Lists were taped to every surface of the lamp. The phone was missing. I frowned, looking for it, then remembered I'd put it into the bottom drawer in a rage two hours before. I pulled it out so I could begin returning the calls that had come in during my half-hour absence.

The office was hot. I went to the barred window that overlooked the lawn and pushed up the old-fashioned latch, but before I could open the window, the loose latch fell back into place, pinching my fingers. I swore softly and moved the latch again, this time holding it until I swung the heavy panes outward. The move and, now, our opening festivities were making me short-tempered and somewhat accident-prone. When things were quiet again, I'd have to try to take it easier. There was no point in becoming a nervous wreck over my job.

When my phone calls were done, I picked up my list of things to check with Frank and went out to Maria's desk. A delicate girl with straight black hair that fell to her waist, she was hunched over the typewriter, one hand pressed to her forehead.

"Maria? Do you have a headache too?"

She looked up, eyes full of tears. "No." Her lower lip pushed out in a pout.

"What's wrong?" Maria's life was a continual series of crises—perhaps because she was so intensely self-centered. She was a good enough secretary, but there were times when I found her humorless self-absorption very tiring.

"My uncle—he is making me go to the Cinco de Mayo party with Robert."

El Cinco de Mayo—May fifth—marks the day in 1862 when the Mexican army defeated the invading French forces at the town of Puebla, near Vera Cruz. The victory was accomplished against incredibly high odds, and the would-be conquerors were driven back to Vera Cruz and the sea. The holiday has taken on special significance for Mexican-Americans, becoming a symbol of their growing cultural awareness and pride, and for that reason we had scheduled our opening gala for the night of May fifth, only three days from now.

I said, "Well, Maria, Robert's nothing to cry over. Didn't you say he usually drinks too much and falls asleep when you and Frank and your aunt double-date?"

She nodded.

"Maybe he'll do that at the party—too much tequila. Then you can dance with Jesse."

Her eyes narrowed. "Robert will fall asleep, yes. But my uncle, he never sleeps."

It was true. I could think of no additional words of comfort. "Where is your uncle, by the way?"

She gestured disgustedly toward Frank's office. "Outside in the garden. The nursery, they delivered some more bushes. He is planting them."

I went into the office and looked out through the window. Beyond its heavy wrought-iron bars was a small courtyard enclosed by an eight-foot-high whitewashed wall. A flagstone path led from the courtyard down the side of the building to the parking lot, where it ended at an ornate gate that matched the style of the window bars. Frank squatted in the center of the courtyard, laboring over a large azalea plant. He was wiring it to a shiny green stake. The plants—I could count seven of them—must have cost a fortune. Even the stakes looked expensive, painted rather than the usual rough wood variety. I wondered if our board of directors had approved the purchase.

Maria came in and stood beside me. She watched Frank a moment, then let out her breath in an angry hiss.

"I don't think I'll bother him right now," I said. "He seems . . . contented."

"He is the only one." Maria turned and started out.

At the door we came face to face with Vic Leary, the museum's business manager. A big, ugly, sad-faced man, he was the only member of Frank's Mafia that I liked. Perhaps it was his air of indefinable sorrow, or perhaps his fiftyish, fatherly concern toward the female staff members and volunteers—whatever, I felt curiously drawn to him. Vic looked from me to Maria and back again.

"Where's Frank?" he asked.

I motioned toward the window.

Vic went up and peered out. "He'll give himself sunstroke, working out there at midday." Vic had been with Frank in his various ventures for more than twenty years, and he was as protective of him as he was of the museum's women. "We'd better tell him to get in here."

"Oh, come on, Vic. He's happy out there. And it keeps him from getting underfoot," I said.

Vic grinned, his homely face twisting. "He's been underfoot a lot lately, hasn't he?"

"Like a little kid with a brand-new house to play in."

"Well, we're going to have to disturb him. And you, too."

"Why?"

"Go out to the parking lot. You'll see. There's a surprise." Vic didn't look too happy about it.

"Pleasant or unpleasant?"

He hesitated. "Depends on your point of view. You'll see. Go ahead. I'll get Frank."

I hurried out to the parking lot, Maria following. There by the loading dock stood a flatbed truck. A ten-foot-high wooden crate was braced in its bed, and a scruffy-looking man, presumably the driver, was prying the crate open. I went around to the other side of the truck where Jesse and Tony Ibarra stood. Isabel Cunningham, a member of our board of directors and our most active volunteer, was up in the flatbed, directing the uncrating.

"Qué pasa?" I asked Jesse.

He shrugged. "Isabel has a surprise for you."

I glanced up at the board member. Isabel was a descendant of one of the old Spanish land-grant families who had controlled a huge rancho east of Santa Barbara in the nineteenth century. She had married into one of the town's wealthiest Anglo families, thus adding to her own consid-

erable fortune. In the immaculate white tennis dress that
was her standard daytime garb, her gray hair perfectly
coiffed, she presented a strange contrast to the driver.
Isabel was not a woman you expected to find in the bed of
a truck.

Frank and Vic came up and joined us. *"Qué pasa?"*
Frank asked.

"What's happening?" Vic echoed.

This time Jesse, Tony, Maria, and I all shrugged.

There was a sound of wood splintering. The driver
dropped his crowbar and eased the front of the crate down.
Isabel turned triumphantly to us.

Inside was an *árbol de la vida*—a tree of life. It was at
least eight feet tall and over four feet wide. The tree has
been, since ancient Mexico, a symbol of life, death, and
rebirth. Most of the older ones are subtly beautiful repre-
sentations of these eternal verities—but they were created
before the advent of acrylic paints.

This particular tree was pink, purple, and green; orange,
turquoise, and yellow; red and blue with gilt accents. Its
ceramic branches contained the Father, the Son, the Virgin
Mary and, for all I knew, the Holy Ghost. Adam and Eve
were there, clutching bright green fig leaves. There were
angels with banjos, horns, harps, and swords. A sun and
moon on either side wore sappy grins. There were horses,
camels, goats, pigs, rabbits, and a lion with a gilt crown.
There were deer, antelopes, panthers, unicorns, and
upside-down doves. In the center, between Adam and Eve,
the head of a serpent emerged from the foliage, munching
on a blue and yellow apple. It was also a flowering tree,
and from each garish blossom red berries stuck out on long
stems, like springs.

Yes, indeed, this tree symbolized it all and more. For all I knew, it glowed in the dark.

"Who on earth did this to us?" I asked in an awed whisper.

Jesse put a hand on my arm. "Hush."

"No, I want to know."

He pointed at Isabel.

I should have known. Isabel was well bred and possessed exquisite taste, except for one idiosyncracy. She loved the modern-day Tree of Life and supported several potters in the town of Metepec, where the trees are primarily made. I suspected, since she was so clearly proud of it, that this one had been perpetrated by one of her protégés. Why, I wondered, did our museum's most generous benefactor have to have this strange streak?

Isabel's triumphant look became questioning. "It's a surprise, for the opening," she said. "Do you like it?"

We all remained speechless.

"Pablo Gomez made it," she added. "It's one of a kind, especially for this museum. There'll never be another like it."

So I had been right; Pablo was her favorite protégé, an old man who turned out these monstrosities the way a fry cook turns out burgers.

Frank recovered first. "It's splendid, Isabel. Just splendid." He turned to me. "Isn't it splendid?" His scowl said I'd better come up with something good; the museum depended on Isabel's contributions.

"It's lovely, Isabel. Such an excellent example of the *árbol de la vida*. And so large. It's so much larger than anything in our collection." I turned to Jesse.

"Yes," he said quickly, "it certainly is large. It must have cost a fortune."

"Price was no object." Isabel waved a hand airily, her uncertainty banished.

"I can't tell you how much we appreciate this, Isabel," Frank said. He turned to Tony this time.

Tony gave his lounge-lizard smirk. "I will take oh-so-many pictures and make new materials for the education."

Now what did that mean? I frowned at him.

"It's beautiful, isn't it, Maria?" Frank said.

Maria gave him a sulky look, then smiled brilliantly at Jesse.

Now it was Frank's turn to frown.

Isabel beamed at us. "Yes, price was no object. Nothing is too good for our opening in our new quarters."

A horrible suspicion crept over me. Did Isabel expect this . . . creation to be in place for the Cinco de Mayo party?

"And, of course, the press preview," she added.

"I—" Panicky, I glanced at Frank. He looked blankly at me. "I—" I cleared my throat. "Isabel, I don't think we can get it in place by then. The preview's tomorrow morning at ten. The other exhibits will have to be shifted to prepare a space large enough . . ."

Isabel frowned. Although charming, she could be difficult when crossed.

"Frank," I said, "I don't think—"

"Do it," Frank said.

"What?"

"Shift the exhibits and get the tree in place."

"But—"

"The folk art gallery is plenty large enough. We can use

a plywood base. Get that painter—what's his name—
Pedro over here. He can paint the wood in colors to high-
light those purple and green flowers." Frank gestured at
the tree. "We can flank it with those two smaller *árboles*
from the permanent collection."

"Frank!" It would take all day to shift the exhibits. The
painter probably would not be available. And who was
going to build this plywood base? Besides, the damned
thing was *ugly*!

Frank, however, had made up his mind. "Tony, take
Isabel into the gallery and help her pick a spot for it."

Tony nodded and slouched over to the truck. He helped
Isabel down and ushered her into the museum.

"Frank!"

Frank stepped up to me, his eyes narrowed to slits.
"Now, listen, you, and listen careful. That tree is going to
be in there in time for the preview."

"Frank, it is gross, it is ugly, it is too damned *big*!"

"You're prejudiced. I know you hate the things."

It was true. I was perfectly willing to admit prejudice.
But it was a prejudice founded on solid artistic principles.
Since the invention of acrylic paints, the trees had become
more and more garish, their branches laden with objects
that had little to do with the combined Indian and Christian
beliefs. I would gladly have displayed one of the older
trees, but not this thing. It was on a par with a piñata from
Tijuana. "That particular tree," I said, "would prejudice
anyone."

"It is going to be displayed whether you like it or not."

"You may be director here, but I'm responsible for the
collections. I am responsible for what people see and don't
see. I am responsible for what they think of Mexican art."

"And you will be responsible for setting that"—he waved wildly at the *árbol*—"up!"

"I will not be responsible for that monstrosity. It's hideous."

"Do it!"

"No, dammit!"

Frank came closer until his nose was a scant six inches from mine. This was the tactic he always used in our frequent arguments. "Yes, dammit," he said softly. "You will do it. That woman in there is worth several million dollars, even now that she'd divorced. That woman in there devotes herself to this museum. That woman in there is not to be crossed.

"Money! Is that all you can think of—money?"

"Money is what keeps us going."

"What about artistic integrity?"

"That is a side issue."

"Not to me, it's not."

"Go in there and get ready to set up that tree."

"There isn't time."

"Nonsense. Vic can build the base for it. He's good with a hammer." Vic jerked in surprise. "If we can't get Pedro, Jesse can paint. After all, he's an artist." Jesse opened his mouth, but no sound came out. "The driver can help us haul the tree into place."

"My orders are only as far as the loading dock," the driver said.

Frank ignored him. He looked back at the tree, his eyes calculating. "We'll set it up, flanked by those two little *árboles*. Stick in some of the fertility symbols and . . . I've got it! We'll put that little terra-cotta tree of death on a pedestal."

"The tree of death!" I said.

"Yes. The tree of death."

"You can't do that! It's unaesthetic. It's not done. It's sacrilege!"

"Do it!"

I felt my rage rising. Take it easy, Elena, I told myself. Watch that temper.

"Is that clear?" Frank added.

I clenched my fists. I gritted my teeth.

"Is it, Miss Oliverez?" He stood there before me, smug and self-satisfied.

"You son of a bitch!" I said. "You *hijo de puta*! What the hell right do you have to mess with my collections?"

Frank took a step back.

"You wander around here for weeks, doing nothing but fiddling with the plants. You sit and brag while everybody else does the work. And now, when the collections are all set and we're ready to go, you decide to switch everything around." I felt Jesse's restraining hand on my arm, but it was too late for caution.

"And for what?" I demanded, now advancing on Frank. "For what, eh? For that?" I motioned wildly at the *árbol*. "It's all the stereotypes about junky Mexican art rolled into one. It'll make the museum look like a cheap souvenir shop. We might as well hang up a piñata or two and some of those bullfighter pictures painted on velvet. Shall we do that, Frank? Do you want to make us a laughing-stock?"

Frank took another step back, but then stood firm. "I said, Miss Oliverez, do it!"

"*Hijo de puta!* Somebody ought to kill you!" I whirled and ran up the steps to the loading dock.

Two

STRANGELY ENOUGH, MY OUTBURST MOVED EVERYONE TO pitch in and help. Maybe it was the satisfaction of hearing me tell Frank off; maybe it was fear that the opening would be spoiled. Probably it was both. But suddenly everyone—except Frank, of course—plunged into activity.

Vic and Jesse corned me in my office and calmed me with words and a beer from the corner store. Isabel announced she had found just the place in the folk art gallery for the *árbol* and went off to buy paint. Even Tony managed to restrain his smirk as he set off to get plywood, a hammer, and some nails. Maria used the time to cast sultry looks at Jesse.

Frank wandered through the office wing twice, pointedly ignoring me but frowning at my beer. Finally he closeted himself in his own office. I suspected he had gone into the courtyard to play with his plants, and was relieved not to have to deal with him.

When they were sure I wouldn't succumb to any homicidal urges, Jesse and Vic went to the folk art gallery to help Tony build the platforms. Isabel returned with the paint and began supervising, much to the others' annoyance. I sent Maria to the store for more beer and then went to the loading dock to take another look at the tree of life.

It was still there, all right—big and ugly as could be. The truck driver lounged in the cab, listening to country music, his feet extending through one window. He didn't seem to mind the delay. It was, I assumed, one of his more interesting deliveries. I gave the *árbol* a final disgusted glance and went inside to help. If we were to display the horror, it might as well be displayed right.

The platforms had been assembled. I went to the ladies' room and changed to the work clothes I kept there, then found a paintbrush and set to work. Thoughtfully, Isabel had bought a quick-drying latex.

As I worked side by side with Jesse, Vic, and Maria— Tony had been banished on grounds of sloppiness and Isabel had had an appointment with another of her numerous charities—most of my tension dissipated. The afternoon grew hot, and we took frequent beer breaks. Jesse joked and told ribald stories from his seemingly unending repertoire. Maria giggled and, at Jesse's urging, sang us some Mexican folk songs. I was surprised by the fine quality of her voice—another talent wasted while in bondage to Don Francisco. Vic was quiet, but smiled. His happy times, I assumed, were few; he would probably treasure the memory of this easy, companionable afternoon.

By four the paint was dry. Isabel returned to supervise

the placement of the *árbol*. The truck driver forgot his orders—once Isabel slipped him a twenty dollar bill—and good-naturedly helped move it in. He probably wanted to see if there would be more fireworks. When it was in place we all stepped back and viewed it. For a moment there was silence.

Then Isabel sighed. "Perfect."

The rest of us said nothing.

"Isn't it?" She turned a worried look on me.

"It's . . . perfect."

Jesse cleared his throat. "The purple and green of the platforms really pick up the colors of those flowers."

Isabel nodded, any doubt stilled once and for all. Jesse was an artist; he *knew* about things like color.

"I suppose we should get Frank in here to see it," Isabel said. "I'll call him." She started for the door, then stopped. "No, wait. What about the little trees of life?"

"Right." Jesse snapped his fingers. "I'll get them."

"And the tree of death."

"Isabel," I said, "I really have to draw the line at that."

"But, Elena, we've built a platform for it. It will spoil the whole arrangement if we don't use it, and Frank . . ."

I closed my eyes, feeling a headache begin to throb. "Okay. Okay. Come on, Jesse. I'll help you."

We left the gallery, crossing the large central courtyard and office wing to the dark hallway that led to our cellar storeroom. There, in the coolness, Jesse stopped me, hand on my arm. "Look, Elena, I know how you feel about this display. But for the good of the museum, we've got to pull together."

"You think that display's going to do the museum good?"

"It won't do that much harm. You know how openings are. People are more interested in the food and booze than in the art. All you have to do is steer the press clear of the folk art gallery tomorrow and we won't have anything to worry about."

"But what about your *camaleones*? They won't get any press coverage if I do that."

"I don't need publicity that bad."

"And what do we do about that monstrosity afterward, when people come to look seriously?"

Jesse grinned. "Maybe the *árbol* will get broken."

"What are you saying, Señor Herrera?"

He spread his hands wide. "Who knows what the future holds, *mi amiga*?"

I grinned, too. "You know, you're right. You are so right."

We went down the hall to the cellar door and descended cold stone steps into the blackness. Jesse fumbled for the light switch, and a dim orange bulb came on. The cellar resembled a fun house maze, with a jumble of packing cases stretching away into the shadows at the far end. Some crates were empty, some were not; in the rush to prepare for the opening, I hadn't had time to unpack what we weren't going to use.

"My first priority once things quiet down," I said, "is this cellar."

Jesse looked around. "As a storage area, it's not bad, though. It keeps cool so you don't have to worry about temperature control, and there's plenty of room. Needs better lighting, of course."

The one bulb was the only real light source. There were little high windows, but they opened onto bricked-in pits just below ground level. The pits were topped with iron gratings that didn't permit much direct light to pass through. "Fluorescents," I said. "Fluorescents as soon as possible. And eventually with ultraviolet shields. If the board can approve Frank buying all those plants, they can't quibble over a few light fixtures. Come on. I think I remember where the *árboles* are."

Jesse and I wrestled with the packing cases and found the *árboles*. The two little trees of life were more tasteful than Isabel's gift but still too garish for my taste—which was why they weren't on display. The tree of death was bland by comparison, two feet tall and of unpainted terra-cotta. Its red-brown branches held a few leaves and no flowers. In the center a grim skeleton sat, surrounded by five skulls. It was not a cheerful sight, but somehow a less unsettling one than the riot of color up in the folk art gallery. We lugged all three trees upstairs, where we found the others, including Frank and Tony, waiting in front of the offending *árbol*. Frank once again avoided my eyes, talking in low tones to Vic until the trees were in place. Then he stepped back, surveyed the scene, and nodded complacently.

"Wonderful, Isabel," he announced. "Just wonderful. Such a generous gift. Such a magnificent beginning in our new quarters. And I'd like to thank you—Tony, Jesse, Vic, and Maria—for doing such a splendid job." Then he turned and marched from the room.

Isabel looked at me and shrugged sympathetically. Jesse patted me on the shoulder. Tony smirked, but his heart wasn't in it. Maria gave her uncle's back a contemptuous glance. I looked at Vic and was surprised at what I saw. He was watching Frank leave, his large fists balled at his sides, his homely face twisted in anger. It was an expression I'd never seen Vic wear, an emotion I hadn't supposed he possessed. Quickly I turned my eyes back to the garish display.

It was nearly five. The others said their goodbyes and began leaving. The truck driver, now twenty dollars richer, accepted a couple of beers and drove off. Only Isabel lingered.

"Is everything set for the buffet tomorrow, Elena?" she asked. She seemed unsure again, and I felt sorry for her. Her gift had been well meant and had brought nothing but trouble.

"Almost. We have the orange juice and champagne. The strawberries are being prepared by a couple of your volunteers. We've got coffee and cheese and bread and . . . oh, damn!"

"What?"

"The sour cream. I was afraid it would spoil, so I was going to pick it up tonight. And I've still got to do my laundry and pay some bills before they come take me away. . . . "

Isabel brightened. She had always been one of those women who need to be needed, and the trait had become more pronounced since her divorce a year ago. "I'll take care of the sour cream."

"Are you sure you want to? You've done so much already."

"I'm sure." She nodded firmly. "And now I think I'll go have a few words with Frank. Where do you suppose he went?"

"His office or the courtyard outside it. The plants, you know."

Isabel looked grim. "Yes, the plants, of course. I'll see you tomorrow morning, then."

Isabel left, and I turned back to the *árbol*. "You just might get broken," I whispered. "Yes, you might." Then, relishing the quiet that had descended, I made a quick check of the other galleries. Everything was in place; everything looked right. I made an adjustment here, flicked at some dust there. I knew I'd check the galleries once more tomorrow morning and still find nothing wrong. But I couldn't help it. This was the first opportunity I'd had to show what I could do. When the press entered my museum it had to look right.

My museum! How Frank would sneer at that. But it was mine, by virtue of the sweat and love I'd invested here. And no fat, lazy Tío Taco was going to ruin it.

Unfortunately, I should check with Frank before leaving, to see if he wanted me to set the alarms. We had no security staff, and our collections' sole protection was the barred windows and a simple household alarm system on the doors. Still, it was an improvement over our previous quarters, where we'd had no alarms at all. I was proud of the new system; I'd fought hard to get an adequate one installed when we'd moved here. Now I could rest better at night, knowing our collections were safe.

I went through the offices, stopped at Frank's, and knocked softly. There was no answer. The office was empty, but in the courtyard his stocky form leaned over the plant closest to the little barred window. He was alone; Isabel's few words with him must have been few indeed.

Frank straightened, wiping dirt from his palms onto his dark blue pants. He stopped, studying the plants, then nodded. When he came in, he didn't notice me.

I cleared my throat.

Frank whirled. His eyes narrowed. "What do you want?"

"Are you leaving soon?"

"Is that any business of yours?"

I sighed. "All I want to know is whether I should set the alarm or if you want to do it."

"You lock up." He turned away.

"Then you're leaving right away?"

"No. I plan to work late, on the budget, and I don't want someone walking in here when I'm not looking."

He could have locked up himself. All he had to do was throw the alarm's inside toggle switch on the wall beside the courtyard door. But, no, I would have to get out my keys and turn on the alarm beside the front entrance. And then, he'd probably forget to reset it when he left. That had happened before.

"Well?" Frank said.

I glanced at the hook midway between the window and the patio door. Frank's ring with the alarm system key and the key to the padlock on the patio gate hung there. He was so absentminded he had to hang his key ring up every morning or he might lose it in his wanderings through the premises. Of course, if he stayed at his desk and worked, that would be less of a danger.

"Don't worry." Frank's eyes had followed mine. "I won't forget to reset it."

"Good."

"And Miss Oliverez. . . ."

"Yes?"

"After the opening you'd better start looking for another place of employment."

He'd threatened to fire me before, so his words didn't surprise me. "Sure, Frank." I turned to go.

"I'm serious. I've already talked to my Colombian about taking over your position."

Slowly I turned back. "Tony? You've got to be kidding."

He assumed an aggressive stance. "Tony is qualified. He has been education director for over six months now."

"And he knows nothing about Mexican art. He hasn't done a thing as education director, and everybody knows it. You yourself generally call him your 'stupid Colombian.' Besides, the board would never approve his appointment."

"The board approved his initial appointment."

"That was on your recommendation. They didn't know him. Now they do, and they'll never—"

"That will be all, Miss Oliverez."

"You know what, Frank?"

"I said, that will be all."

"I don't regret what I said to you out on the loading dock. I don't regret a word of it." And before it could erupt into one of our full-scale arguments, I left the office. When I went to set the alarm, I was so angry that my hands shook and I could barely turn the key from the up to the down position. That done, I almost ran to my car. Home. I needed to go home.

Of course, traffic was terrible. I sat behind the wheel of the Rabbit, fuming and muttering. Just let Frank try to put Tony in my job. All it would do was prove to the board that he was a certifiable lunatic. He ought to be stopped before he did irreparable damage to the museum. He ought to be . . .

A horn honked behind me. I gestured angrily, tried to shift the Rabbit into gear too quickly, and stalled. By the time I got it started, the light had changed.

Maybe I *should* look for another job. The problems at the museum were sapping my energy. I was there to care for our collections, dammit, not act as referee for a bunch of quarrelsome, petty . . .

This time I was ready for the light. I shot through it, heading crosstown.

Santa Barbara is a seaside city of around 75,000, stretching north along the coast to the University of California, my alma mater, and south to Montecito, where the rich people live. The shoreline curves along the Pacific, edged with beaches and parks. To the east, softly rounded hills form a protective bowl. The beauty of the natural setting is further enhanced by the graceful Spanish architecture, which reflects the town's heritage. Santa Barbara has become one of the foremost vacation areas in California and is a haven for the wealthy and famous, many of whom are seeking to escape the cheap glitter of Hollywood to the south. My house was not in one of their exclusive neighborhoods, but midway between the hills and the shore, in the closest thing we have to a barrio.

The neighbors' kids were playing ball in the street, the way I'd played there years before. I pulled into my driveway, waved to them, and went up on the front porch. The house was a typical green stucco California bungalow. The thick palm tree in the front yard and the fuschia that ran wild over the porch did much to disguise it, but the fact remained that one of these days I was going to have to shell out for a new paint job. I took my mail from the box—three more bills—and went inside.

The day's heat had built up in there. I opened the windows on the front and side of the living room, kicked off my shoes, and set the bills on my little desk. There was something I had to take care of. What? Oh, yes, the car re-registration. There it was, in the pigeonhole where I kept urgent papers. The pigeonhole was crammed full. I wrote a check to the Department of Motor Vehicles and sealed it in the envelope. Whatever else was urgent could wait until after the opening.

Then I went to the old-fashioned kitchen, got a glass of cool white wine, and came back to the living room. I sat down in a rocker by the side window, enjoying the breeze. The late afternoon sun cast long shadows on the polished hardwood floors, and the thin white curtains billowed. For the first time today I felt at peace.

This house was my haven, the place I felt most comfortable in all the world. It ought to be; I'd been born in this house, raised here, lived here all my life. Up until six years ago, when I'd finished college, my mother had lived here, too. Then, the day after my graduation from UCSB, she'd announced she was going to sell.

Why? I'd asked her. Because both of her girls were through college and she was going to retire.

That was understandable. Mama had worked as a domestic for the city's wealthiest families—including Isabel Cunningham—ever since my father died when I was only three. She'd managed to buy the house, put money away, and help both me and my older sister Carlota through college. For us, the tradition of machismo, so prevalent in most Mexican-American homes, had died with my father. The women in the Oliverez household had to be strong and independent, according to Mama. We made our way in the world, refusing to let anyone, male or female, put us down. And she was the strongest.

My mother had worked hard; it was natural she should want—and deserve—to retire. But why sell the house?

Well, Mama explained, there was this mobile home park up in Goleta, near the beach. They had a swimming pool and a recreation center and a crafts workshop. They organized trips to plays and the symphony, and every Saturday night there was a barbecue. A mobile home would be much easier to keep up than this house. And besides—this with a wicked gleam in her eye—most of the people were around her age. There would be widowers.

Mama! I had exclaimed.

What did I expect? she demanded. She'd been without a man long enough. Of course, it wasn't anything she thought I would understand. I hadn't been without one since I was old enough to flirt.

That stilled my objections, and made me think. All those years Mama had been alone. And Carlota and I had been running here and there—parties, summer vacations—without so much as a thank you or a thought of her loneliness. Of course she should have her mobile home. But I asked her not to put the house on the market just yet.

Then I called Carlota in Minneapolis, where she was an assistant professor of sociology at the University of Minnesota. We worked it out that she would buy the mobile home and I would make the rental payments on the space for it. In return, Mama would deed the house to us. I would maintain it and live there, and if I ever wanted to buy her out, Carlota would agree to it. Within a month Mama had moved, and two weeks after that, she had a boyfriend. I am definitely my mother's daughter.

The nice thing about the mobile home park was that it had a laundry. And, since I couldn't afford a washer and dryer yet, I paid the laundry frequent visits.

Now I finished my wine, went to my bedroom and collected my dirty clothes. On the way out I called my mother.

"It's laundry night," I said. "Do you want me to bring anything?"

"I could use some milk."

"Anything else?"

"Dinner is chile verde. Nick is coming, but there's plenty for you. I'm low on lettuce, though. And maybe some of those nice avocados they're bringing up from Mexico? What do you think of a tomato and avocado salad? With some sweet onion. Yes, a couple of tomatoes and one onion, a large one. And—"

"Just a minute. I've got to get a pencil." I wrote down those and several more requests, then set off for the shopping center. It was small price to pay for getting the laundry done and enjoying some good company.

THREE

As I CAME OUT OF THE SAFEWAY PUSHING MY CART, ISABEL'S tan Mercedes pulled up. I felt a stab of embarrassment. I had made myself sound so busy, but there I was at the store. I could have bought the sour cream. Isabel saw me and hurried up. Her gray-streaked hair straggled from its bun, and there was a brownish dirt smudge on her usually immaculate white tennis dress. My embarrassment turned to pity; after all the hours she toiled for the museum, we had scorned her gift.

"Isabel," I said quickly, "I'm sorry. I didn't realize I'd have to stop at Safeway, but my mother needed some things. If I'd known, I would have bought the sour cream."

She brushed the apology aside with a flick of her hand. "That's all right. How is your mother, anyway?"

"She's fine."

"Good, good. Actually, I'm glad I ran into you. Don't

you think we should have sugar as well as sour cream for the guests to dip the strawberries in?"

"That's not a bad idea."

"Both brown and powdered sugar."

"Yes. Do we have any dishes to put it in, though?"

"I have some silver bowls at home. I'll bring them."

"You're so good to us."

Again, she flicked her hand. "*De nada*. I like my work for the museum. Unlike a few other charities I could name. I met with that restoration group this afternoon—you know, the one that's trying to get the old Sanchez property. They have no idea what it takes in terms of organization. . . . " She launched into a long, distracted account of the troubles she had encountered with the group, then began telling me about the impractical outlook of a church group that was assisting illegal aliens. I shifted from foot to foot, leaning on my grocery cart. Isabel didn't seem to notice my impatience, and I didn't have the heart to interrupt. The woman had obviously had a rough day, and it was in part my fault. When she finally ran down, I loaded my groceries in my car and drove to Goleta.

I parked in a visitor's slot near the spacious lawn in front of the redwood and shingle recreation center of the mobile home park. Beyond the building were a pool and a putting green, and the trailers stood on U-shaped culs-de-sac around this central area. Each had its own little yard and shade tree.

The smell of chile verde—pork and beef chunks simmering with green chiles and spices—filled my mother's trailer. She and her latest boyfriend, Nick Carrillo, sat in the living room drinking white wine. I got myself a glass and joined them.

"So what's new with you, Miss Elena?" Nick asked. "You ready to take up running yet?" He was a tall, white-haired man of seventy-eight who jogged several miles a day. He was always trying to get me interested in running, but to no avail.

"I told you, I'm the sedentary type."

"You were on the women's swimming team in college."

"That's different. I'm good at swimming."

"Then you'd be good at running."

That was probably true. I had a very slow heartbeat and when I swam it slowed down even more and my endurance grew. It would work the same if I ran. But I didn't want to run. Besides, if I started running, Nick and I would have nothing to argue about.

"Sorry, Nick."

"You ought to do something about exercise," Mama said.

"You're a fine one to talk. You hate to exercise, and look at you—you're as slim as I am." My mother was the youngest-looking woman of sixty-seven I'd ever seen. In fact, except for her hair being straight and gray instead of curly and dark brown, she and I looked a lot alike. We had the same regular features, and hers were almost as unlined as mine. Only her hands attested to her lifetime of hard work.

"I'm talking about exercising for your health, not your figure," Mama said. "You don't look so good today."

"Now, Gabriela, leave the girl alone," Nick cautioned.

"I'm just tired." I took a sip of wine. "The museum—"

"You need food." My mother stood up. "Go put your laundry in. Nick will help me with the salad."

I went to the laundry room in the recreation center and

stuffed my clothes in the machine. When I got back to the trailer, the table was set and Mama was ladling out the chile verde and rice. "Sit and eat," she said.

Over dinner Nick asked. "That Frank still giving you trouble?"

"Always. Now he's threatening to fire me and give my job to the Colombian."

"Isn't the Colombian some kind of moron?"

"Yes. Frank doesn't mean it . . . I don't think."

Mama frowned. "What did you do to Frank to make him threaten that?"

"Why is it always *my* fault? Why do you think I did something to him?"

"I know you."

"Mama, that's not fair!"

"Ladies, ladies," Nick said.

"All right, maybe you're right. Maybe I did do something to Frank. But it was justified."

"What did you do?"

"I . . . uh . . . I told him someone should kill him. And I called him a terrible name. In front of everybody."

Mama looked triumphantly at Nick. "See?"

"Well," Nick said in a conciliatory tone, "he must have done something to cause that."

"You bet he did!" I told them in gruesome detail about the tree of life.

Mama sighed. "Isabel. She means well, poor thing."

"Poor thing!" I said. "She has millions."

"And nothing else."

"That's true. She threw old Doug Cunningham out after he started playing around with that twenty-five-year-old model."

"Well, Douglas was no prize even before that. Isabel could have done far better. She was a Vallejo, you know."

During the three decades of Mexican rule in the 1800s, a landed gentry had emerged in Alta California. Spanish by birth, most often soldiers who had served loyally, the dons who founded such aristocratic lines as the Vallejos were granted huge tracts of pastureland by the government. On them they raised horses, cattle, and sheep and built elaborate haciendas. The elegant life-style of the ranchos has been romanticized in story and song and even now is recreated in yearly celebrations such as Santa Barbara's Fiesta Days. Isabel had indeed descended from a privileged background.

"No," my mother said, "Isabel didn't have to marry the likes of Douglas Cunningham."

I poured myself more wine. "What? You think she shouldn't have married an Anglo?" Mama didn't approve of mixed marriages, and she was ominously silent whenever I dated an Anglo.

"I didn't say that."

"You meant it."

"Ladies," Nick said.

"Maybe you think she should have married someone like Frank De Palma?" I smiled as I said it, picturing the immaculate Isabel trying to reform Frank.

My mother's face, however, was serious. "Certainly not. A marriage like that would have destroyed her."

"What do you mean?"

"Look at Frank. If anyone ever lived the tradition of machismo, he is it. Frank demands complete obedience from his women. He would have broken the spirit of someone like Isabel."

"But Isabel was raised in that tradition, too. You should see the way she defers to Frank at the museum."

"That's at the museum. I'm talking about in the home. A man like Frank would have driven Isabel mad. At least with an Anglo she could let her anger loose and divorce him."

"So why are you always hinting I should marry one of our own kind? You think someone like Frank wouldn't drive *me* around the bend?"

Mama sighed. "Not all of our men live and breathe machismo. Frank is an extreme. Look what he's done to his wife." Her eyes became faraway, remembering. "Rosa Rivera—as she was called then—was the loveliest girl. Why she married Frank I don't know. He was the grubbiest little boy when we were growing up in the barrio. And he hasn't improved much."

"Well, there's no accounting for tastes."

She looked sternly at me. "*Your* mother would certainly know that."

"My taste isn't so bad!"

"Oh? What about that Steve? The one with the motorcycle?"

"Admittedly, he was a mistake."

"And Jim? All that hair."

"He wasn't so bad!"

"No?"

"Well, he wasn't."

"Yes," she said darkly. "I know what you liked about him."

"Ladies."

"If you mean, was he good in—"

"Ladies!"

Both of us looked at Nick.

"Enough."

Quietly we returned our attention to our plates.

In a few minutes Nick got up and cleared the table for dessert. Fresh fruit. Mama liked sweets, but she didn't dare serve them when the old health nut was around.

Nick wolfed down some grapes and stood up. "I don't mean to run out so fast," he said, "but I've got a meeting at the rec center to plan for the marathon."

"Marathon?" I looked up from the apple I was cutting.

"Yes." His eyes sparkled. "A bunch of us old fogies are organizing a marathon race—show you young folks how to do it right."

I rolled my eyes. "What next?"

"Next I get you out there. Thanks for dinner, Gabriela. Maybe I'll drop back later."

"Do that, Nick."

He went out, and Mama and I sat there in silence. Finally she said, "Is your job really in trouble, Elena?"

I shrugged. "I don't know. Sometimes I feel I should chuck it anyway. The pettiness is getting to me."

"What would you do?"

"I don't know. I'd have to move away. There's not much available in my field in Santa Barbara. And I don't want to do that."

"What, my little girl is not adventurous?"

"Not really. I like it here. I like the house." I looked around the cozy trailer. "I guess I have my mother's nesting instinct."

She looked fondly at me. "Both you girls do. I don't think Carlota would have moved away either, if there hadn't been such a shortage of teaching jobs."

"Probably not. Have you heard from her?"

"On Sunday she called."

"Anything new?"

"No."

I went to switch my laundry to the dryer. On the way through the rec center I spotted Nick and his "old fogies" conferring in the lounge. There seemed to be some disagreement on how the marathon would be run, because they were all talking loudly at once. Nick waved cheerfully at me, though. I guess they enjoyed shouting.

Back at the trailer, I found Mama unfolding a couple of lounge chairs on the little spot of lawn. "Come and sit awhile," she said.

I sat. For a few minutes we didn't speak. Then she said, "Are you sure everything's all right at the museum, Elena?"

She must really be worried. My job had always had its ups and downs, some more serious than today's. "Everything's not all right, but I don't see why you're so concerned."

"I have a feeling."

"Oh, your feelings!" Mama often laid claim to premonitions. When I scoffed at them, she would merely give me a dark look that said, *There are things more terrible here than you can imagine.* Unfortunately, her premonitions were usually right.

"So what do you think is going to happen?" I asked.

"I don't know. It's just a feeling."

She sounded forlorn, and I tried to reassure her. "Okay, what's the worst that can happen? I can lose my job. There are other jobs."

She didn't say anything.

"Okay, suppose the opening's a bust. Or the volunteers forget the strawberries for the press preview. Or Maria elopes with Vic." I decided to joke her out of her mood. "Or maybe Tony will run off with Isabel. A rich person might will us a whole bunch of *árboles de la vida*, uglier than what we've got now. Or Frank will get even fatter. Or I'll elope with rotund Robert." None of it was very funny, however, and Mama wasn't having any cheering up.

"I just have got this feeling."

"Mama, Mama, you're depressing me."

"I don't mean to."

I patted her work-worn hand. "I know."

We sat there in the silence, listening to the crickets and occasional conversations of people passing by. Around ten o'clock Nick reappeared, and I took it as my signal to leave. Collecting my clothes from the dryer, I waved good-bye to the remnants of the group of "old fogies" and went to my car.

I wasn't sleepy. In spite of a straight week of lying awake nights, I wasn't tired at all. I sat in the dark, tapping my fingers on the steering wheel, then started the car and drove toward the museum. All was dark, except for the floodlights on the lawn. For a moment I debated going in, checking the collections once more, but decided against it. I was getting obsessive about my work, and I didn't like that. Finally I drove to the palm-dotted park on Cabrillo Street along the waterfront and sat in my car, watching the lovers on the grass.

I didn't have a male friend right now. Jim—the one who was good in bed—had gone out of my life six months ago, and since then the museum had taken all my time. That wasn't right. I should be getting out, going to parties, meeting people.

But why? Somehow the old game didn't interest me anymore. I would much rather sit in my house reading art journals and novels than go out partying. Maybe I was going to be alone all my life. Maybe I would never find anybody to be comfortable with. Mama never said anything, but I knew she worried about grandchildren. What if she'd raised Carlota and me to be too independent?

Children. Did I want them? I didn't know. Children were such an unknown quantity when the man who would father them was faceless.

A husband? Did I really want anyone on a permanent basis? I didnt' know that either.

Angrily I shook myself. "You're too damn introspective these days, Elena," I said aloud. "No wonder you don't sleep at night."

The words echoed in the little car. Then the sound died, and I felt more alone than ever. Mama had a feeling. Her feelings were usually right. But what did it mean?

I sat there for a long time, until the moon disappeared behind a giant palm tree and the lovers were gone from the grass.

FOUR

MY OUTLOOK, LIKE JESSE'S *CAMALEONES*, CHANGED THE NEXT morning. I felt optimistic, positive. The press preview would be a success, the opening even better. The problems at the museum were not insoluble. Once things quieted down, I would deal with them. And, if they proved more than I could handle, well there were other jobs, weren't there?

I parked in front of the stately adobe and crossed the grass. The alarm, I noted approvingly, was on, although the lock was in the up position, which meant that Frank had left by another door. The fact remained that he had remembered my warning to reset the alarm. It was a good omen.

I went into the central courtyard and turned on the fountain. The water gurgled and sputtered for a moment, then began tinkling happily. Another good omen.

The folding tables for the buffet were stored in the corridor outside Frank's office. I went in there, put away my purse, and started hauling tables to the courtyard. Passing Frank's door, I looked in and spied his keys hanging on the hook. So he was here early. With luck, he'd be reasonably presentable and in a mood to greet the reporters. Deciding to avoid him for now, I moved the folding tables by myself.

By the time Isabel and her other volunteers had arrived, I had covered each table with a white cloth and set out napkins and glasses. The volunteers unveiled huge cut glass bowls of spring strawberries, and I helped Isabel fill the smaller silver bowls with sugar. Vic arrived and began to mix the champagne and orange juice punch. Naturally Frank didn't come out to lend a hand.

By nine-thirty Tony hadn't yet put in an appearance. That didn't bother me; he was often late, and if he didn't show up at all he wouldn't be able to say stupid things to the reporters. What did bother me was Maria's absence. We could have used another pair of hands. And, come to think of it, where was Jesse? He'd promised to be here as a representative of the local artistic community. Maybe the two of them were off having a tryst. Honestly, couldn't I count on anyone?

The hands of my watch showed quarter to ten when we finished laying out the buffet and stood back to admire it. I turned to Vic. "Go in and call Maria. Tell her she's got to hurry. And try Jesse."

He nodded and went into the office wing. A moment later he returned. "Guess they're on the way. No answer at Jesse's, and the line's busy at Frank's."

"Probably one of the *gordicitos* tying up the phone," I said. "I'm going to check the galleries, and then I'll get

Frank." I'd been holding off on the galleries, having decided that controlling my obsessive behavior was a good place for the new, optimistic me to start.

I crossed the courtyard and started through the galleries. They looked good. I flicked at the same imaginary specks of dust as yesterday. Everything shone. Our collections had never looked better. Even that damned *árbol de la vida* might look okay this morning. I reserved judgment; if it didn't, the folk art gallery would be off limits to the press.

I rounded the corner to the gallery, bracing myself for the tree's spectacular ugliness. Then I stopped. The tree was gone.

On the platform where it had stood was a gapping emptiness. The tree was gone. The tree was . . . on the floor. Smashed into hundreds of garish fragments. Shattered. And under it . . .

I put my hand to my mouth, stifling a scream. It came out a strangled grunt.

Under the remains of the tree lay Frank. He was on his face, his arms and legs splayed out. There were dark, dried stains on the floor near where a large section of the tree lay on his head. He was not breathing.

I grasped at the wall for balance. *Por Dios!* How had this happened?

I took a faltering step forward, and something crunched under my foot. Looking down, I saw it was one of the shocking pink flowers. I looked back at Frank, surrounded by the gaudy wreckage, and thought of my words of the day before: *Someone ought to kill you.* Facing the reality of Frank's death, those words seemed reprehensible. No one should speak idly of death. And no one, not even Frank, deserved to die like this.

And then as I stood there, staring at his inert body, I realized what part of the tree had crushed his skull. It was the center, with the red-eyed, fanged serpent.

The scream again rose to my throat. Again I forced it back. The press would be arriving about now. I didn't want them swarming all over here. I didn't want them staring like vultures at Frank's broken body.

What to do?

I backed from the room, my eyes still on Frank, then turned and ran through the gallery to the courtyard. A couple of reporters had already arrived and were eyeing the buffet. Isabel stood by the door. I grabbed her arm.

"Have the volunteers give them some punch. Let them eat," I said.

She nodded, then took a good look at my face. "What's the matter?"

"Nothing. Just keep them amused. Load them up with champagne." I rushed across the courtyard to the office wing.

Vic was hanging up the phone. He turned to me. "Still busy. I don't know where the hell Maria is."

I didn't reply. I was shaking all over. I picked up the receiver and dialed. Thank God for the 911 emergency number. I could not have dialed more digits.

"What are you doing?" Vic asked.

I shook my head. The operator came on. I gave my name and the address of the museum. I said there had been a fatal accident. I said we had press people all over the place. Could the cops attract as little attention as possible?

Vic's eyes widened.

I put down the phone and turned to him.

"Who?" he asked.

"Frank. In the folk art gallery. He must have been fooling with the *árbol de la vida*. It fell on him. Crushed his head."

Vic's face twisted. "Are you sure he's dead?"

"I didn't touch him, but you can tell when someone's not breathing. It's quiet in there, so quiet. . . ." I began to shake harder.

Vic put his arm around me. "Hey, don't do that."

"I . . . can't . . . help . . . it. . . ."

He forced me into a chair. "Take a deep breath."

I complied.

"Does anyone else know?" he asked.

I shook my head. "I told Isabel to keep the reporters amused."

"God. The reporters."

"Right."

Vic stared at me. Then he asked, "You okay now?"

"No. Yes. Better anyway."

"Let me go get some champagne. We both need it."

He left. It was quiet in the offices, too. Much too quiet.

Vic returned with a bottle of champagne. "The straight stuff," he said. "We don't need orange juice." He rummaged around, found two coffee cups and poured. I took one and gulped, the bubbles stinging my nose. Vic drank his down in one swallow, then poured more. I looked at the cup I held. It was decorated with a heart and said "Daddy." I shuddered. It was Frank's; one of his children had given it to him for Father's Day last year. What it had been doing here, on Maria's desk, I didn't know. Frank was so absent-minded. He probably didn't know where he'd left it.

The door to the office wing opened, and Isabel came in, white-faced. "There are policemen here," she whispered.

"Yes." I stood up. "Send them in here. Try not to let the reporters see."

She stood back. Two uniformed patrolmen entered. I set down the mug of champagne and explained what I had found. When I was done, Vic took them off to the gallery.

I sat down again. Poured more champagne. Drank it. I hadn't eaten any breakfast that morning, and I felt light-headed. That was what shock could do to you. Absently I poured more champagne. Lifted the cup to my lips.

"Give me that!" It was Vic. "You're going to get drunk. How will that look to the cops at ten-thirty in the morning?"

I looked up at him and giggled.

"Jesus!" Vic snatched the cup.

I giggled again.

The door opened, and a middle-aged man came in. He was an Anglo, and everything about him was brown—hair, suntanned face, business suit, tie, shoes, even the rims of his sunglasses. He stared at me, and my giggles evaporated.

"Are you the one who reported it?" he asked.

"Yes." I started to get out of my chair, then decided it wouldn't be wise.

"This is Elena Oliverez, our curator," Vic said. "I'm Vic Leary, the business manager."

"Lieutenant Dave Kirk. Homicide." He didn't offer his hand.

"Homicide?" I said and then, indelicately, hiccuped.

"I don't understand," Vic said, glaring at me. "Mr. De Palma was killed by accident. The tree of life—"

"We have to investigate all unusual deaths. Who found him?"

I was sobering fast. "I did."

"Tell me how it happened."

I told him.

Kirk nodded and turned to Vic. "Let's go to the gallery."

Quietly Vic led him from the room.

Homicide. I reached for the coffee cup, which Vic had set on top of a filing cabinet, then changed my mind. Unusual deaths. I got up and went to the courtyard.

There were about twenty reporters and cameramen out there, from both the newspapers and local TV. The bowls of strawberries had been reduced by half, and a volunteer was adding to the punch. Isabel stood by the door to the galleries, guarding it. She jumped when I went up and put a hand on her arm.

"Vic told me," she whispered. "What are we going to do with them?" She motioned at the crowd.

"Keep feeding them champagne. Obviously, the tour is off. Someone will have to make a statement sooner or later.

"Who?"

"Me, probably." It occurred to me that I should call Carlos Bautista, the chairman of our board. I patted Isabel reassuringly and went back to the offices. Then I realized that Carlos was on vacation in Acapulco. Who else to notify? The rest of the board members were fairly ineffectual. Chances were they would panic. It was up to me, I decided.

The door opened, and Lieutenant Kirk came in. He stopped and surveyed me. His eyes were expressionless, his face bland. "The men from the laboratory are on their way," he said. "Is there some place they can come in where the reporters won't notice?"

I thought. "Through the rear courtyard?"

"However."

I led him through Frank's office to the walled patio and, digging in my pocket, took out the key to the padlock on the iron gate. "This passageway leads to the parking lot, near the loading dock." I motioned at the narrow stone walk and the gate. "They can park out there, and no one will notice them coming in."

"Good." He turned to go.

I followed him back across the courtyard. One of the new azalea bushes, the one closest to the office window, had fallen over. The museum was going to pieces already. I looked for the stake to prop it up, but didn't see it, and my eyes blurred with tears. I wasn't crying for Frank; his death didn't alter the fact that I'd hated him. I was crying for the museum, for what this disaster might do to it. And I was crying for myself, too. I didn't know if I would be up to the tasks ahead.

Lieutenant Kirk stopped in the doorway and watched me. I straightened, wiping the tears away. His expression was as blank as before. "You'd better do something about the press people," he said. "We can't have them tramping through the galleries."

"I'll make a statement, send them away." I stepped through the door in front of him and went out to Maria's typewriter, where I composed a brief statement. While I was doing so, the lab technicians passed through the office with their equipment.

By the time I got to the courtyard, the buffet had been decimated and the reporters were beginning to get restless. "They keep asking when the tour starts," Isabel said. "What are we going to do?"

"Cancel it." I went over to the table and rapped on a glass for attention. My eyes fixed on the sheet of paper I held, I read my statement: "It is my sad duty to inform you that the director of the Museum of Mexican Arts, Mr. Francisco De Palma, was killed in an accident in one of our galleries this morning. Because of this tragedy, we will be unable to conduct the tour as planned. I'd like to ask you to leave the premises at this time so the police can finish their business here. You will be contacted about a press conference later."

There were startled exclamations, and then the questions flew. I held up my hand. "I'm sorry. I can't answer any questions right now. Someone will contact you later." Then I fled to the offices.

Vic stood just inside the door. "I finally got through to Frank's home. Jesse and Maria are there. She called him this morning when they realized Frank hadn't come home all night."

Of course, the clothes he was wearing were the same as yesterday's. Where, if not with his family, had he been? "They waited until this morning to start worrying?"

Vic nodded. "Frank . . . uh . . . often didn't come home."

"What does that mean?"

"Just what I said." Vic looked uncomfortable.

I couldn't believe the notion that was dawning on me. "Don't tell me he had something going on the side?"

"Uh, yeah."

"Frank?"

"Yes."

"*Por Dios*, who on earth would—" I stopped. No sense speaking like that to Vic, who had been Frank's friend. Maybe there were women who liked sloppy, overweight little men. After all, my mother had said Rosa De Palma was once a beauty. If he'd managed to win her, it was conceivable. . . . "Vic, if he often stayed away all night, why did they worry this morning?"

"He always got back in time to have breakfast with the kids."

"But why didn't they call the museum, to see if he was here?"

"They did, but got no answer. Then they started calling . . . elsewhere." Vic looked extremely uncomfortable now.

I decided not to pursue it. "How's the family taking it?"

"Badly."

"Do you want to go over there?"

"The cops said not to leave."

"Well, once they're done, we'll close for the day. I'll have to call a meeting of the board, decide about the press conference. Do you know where Carlos Bautista is staying in Acapulco?"

"The number should be somewhere on Frank's desk."

"Good. We need to notify him. We need to . . ."

Lieutenant Kirk came in. He looked a shade grimmer than before. "May I speak with you, Miss Oliverez?"

"Certainly."

"We'll be removing the body shortly. Have you cleared the museum of reporters?"

"They should be gone by now."

"Good. As soon as we're through in there"—he motioned toward the galleries with his thumb—"I want to meet with each employee individually."

"Why?"

"I want to reconstruct when they last saw the deceased."

"Why should that matter?"

He ignored the question. "Please instruct them—and the volunteers—not to leave the premises for any reason."

"But why?"

Again he ignored me. "Since you found the body, I'll begin with you."

"I don't understand all this."

He looked at me, his face unreadable. "This is not merely a routine investigation, Miss Oliverez."

"Why!"

"Because Frank De Palma wasn't killed by accident. He was murdered."

FIVE

I COULDN'T BELIEVE IT. EVEN AFTER I HAD TALKED TO LIEU-tenant Kirk—giving him a detailed statement on every-thing that had happened from the time I got to work the day before to the time I picked up the phone and called the police—I still couldn't believe it.

Frank, the lieutenant told me, had been hit on the head with a heavy object. The police hadn't yet found out what it was. The tree of life had then been pushed over onto his body in a clumsy attempt to cover up the crime.

I had turned over my office to Lieutenant Kirk, so he could talk to each of us in private. As I left, Vic entered, giving me a comforting glance that somehow didn't come off. I wandered out of the office wing. In the folk art gallery, the lab technicians were finishing up. Frank's body had been removed, but there were chalk marks on the floor and the *árbol de la vida* and nearby display cases were

covered with what I assumed was fingerprint powder.
Mechanically I looked around the gallery to see if anything
other than the tree had been damaged. The other displays
looked all right, but I sensed something wrong. What? I
couldn't put my finger on it. What . . . ?

Isabel came up behind me. "Elena?"

"Yes?"

"The phones are ringing constantly. Reporters. I don't
know what to tell them."

"Just what I did—that we'll call a press conference later.
I have to talk to Carlos, and I'd better do that now." We left
the gallery and went back across the courtyard. "You take
care of the phones," I told Isabel and went into Frank's
office.

It was exactly as it had been the afternoon before. Sun-
light slanted through the window, throwing the shadow of
the iron bars across the clean desk. A tidy desk, in Frank's
case, had been no virtue. It was always like that and, more
often than not, the padded leather chair was unoccupied.

I sat down and opened the center drawer of the desk.
Nothing there but pens and pencils. The pencils were all
pointed and sharp. In a side drawer I found the budget
sheets Frank had said he was going to work on last night. I
doubted that story; Vic prepared the budget, and Frank
took his advice. He'd merely said that so I would think he
was doing something.

I flipped through the ledger sheets. They were covered
with Vic's neat figures. The last one, however, was
scrawled in Frank's bolder hand. Maybe he had done some
work after all. I scanned the sheet.

It was a list of names with numbers opposite them. The
names were unfamiliar to me, and the numbers were much

too large to have anything to do with the museum budget: $50,000; $61,500. If only we had that many grants of that amount!

So it must be a personal ledger sheet. What did it mean? Prices of houses Frank was looking at? He'd been talking about moving recently. No, they were much too low for Santa Barbara's real estate. Debts? Surely Frank hadn't been that far in the red. Gambling debts? Maybe he'd had a secret vice. The thought pleased me, but I shrugged and replaced the ledger sheets. It wasn't my business, especially now that he was dead. Flipping through the desk calendar, I finally found the number of Carlos Bautista's hotel in Acapulco and reached for the phone.

One of the buttons was lit and another flashing. Isabel was obviously having trouble keeping up with the calls. I punched the flashing button and said, "Museum of Mexican Arts."

"Elena? Is that you?" It was Susana Ibarra, Tony's teenage bride. With a start, I remembered Tony hadn't put in an appearance that morning.

"Yes, Susana."

"What are you doing answering the phone?"

"Maria's not here."

"Is she sick?"

Impatiently, I tapped my fingers on the desk blotter. Susana was a silly girl, the perfect teenage vamp. She wore her skirts too short, her makeup too heavy, and her long dark hair extravagantly teased. She chewed gum constantly and, if given the opportunity, would babble on for hours, punctuating her conversation with shrill giggles. "No, Susana," I said, "Maria's not sick."

"Well, that's good because there's something terrible

going around. First I had it and now Tony. That is why I'm calling, to say Tony won't be in to work today."

That was nothing new. She frequently called in with excuses for Tony. He didn't appear sickly, but he was out at least five days of every month.

"You haven't heard the news, then," I said.

"News?"

"Frank's dead. Somebody murdered him in the folk art gallery."

There was a gasp, then silence.

"Susana, are you there?"

"I am . . . here."

"Maybe I better talk to Tony."

"No! You can't."

"Why not? He *is* there, isn't he?"

"Yes . . . he is . . . but he can't come to the phone. He's sick. That is, he's throwing up and he can't . . . I will have him call back." She hung up.

I stared at the receiver for a moment, then replaced it. For the first time ever, something I had said had gotten through to Susana. I only hoped she'd be able to communicate it to Tony before she went off into babbling hysterics. I sighed, then direct-dialed Carlos Bautista's hotel in Mexico.

Carlos, an amiable, shrewd-minded man who had made a fortune in oil, was shocked but calm. He told me to refer the press to the police for information; he would cut his vacation short and return tonight; we would hold a board meeting as soon as he arrived. "In the meantime," he added, "I'm appointing you acting director. You can hold your press conference and tell them that, no more."

"Me? Acting director?"

"Yes, you. Why not? You're the only one there who appears to be doing anything."

"Well, I'm honored, of course. Do you think perhaps we should cancel the Cinco de Mayo party?"

There was a pause. "No, I don't. Vic tells me we've sold a large number of tickets for it. There will be almost as many more sold at the door. We can't afford to cancel the party—or to lose the support and enthusiasm of those people. We'll go ahead with it."

"All right. I'll see you tonight."

I hung up the phone, imagining a heavy weight descending onto my shoulders. Days ago I would have given anything to be running the museum. Now the thought of it just made me tired.

"What are you doing in here?" It was Lieutenant Kirk, and he looked furious.

"Calling our board chairman."

"Don't you know better than to mess with the deceased's desk before I've had a chance to go through it?"

"All I did was use the phone!"

"That doesn't matter. Come on. I need to talk to you anyway."

I stood up, feeling even more tired. "I told you everything I know."

He looked at me. Again, I couldn't read his expression. "Did you?"

"Yes."

"Then we'll go over it once more. Certain inconsistencies in your statement have come to light."

Inconsistencies? What did that mean? I followed Kirk back to my own office.

The office smelled of cigarette smoke, and the ashtray

was full of butts. A coffee cup sat on a stack of papers. Kirk certainly was making himself at home. The lieutenant plunked himself in my swivel chair, and I sat down across the desk from him, feeling displaced.

"What did your board chairman say?" he asked.

"That we're to refer press questions to your department. I'll tell them at the press conference."

"Why have one at all?"

"I'm also to announce that I've been named acting director."

"Acting director? Come up in the world, haven't you?"

I looked sharply at him, but his face was blank.

"All right." He consulted a legal pad on the desk in front of him. "I see here that a couple of your people are not on the premises. Mr. Ibarra. . . ."

"Tony's at home sick. His wife called in. He's supposed to call me back."

Kirk nodded. "And Miss De La Cruz?"

"She and Mr. Herrera are at the De Palma home."

"Mr. Herrera?"

"He's an artist. Actually he isn't on staff, but he was supposed to be here for the press preview. He's one of our best known contemporary exhibitors."

"You have home addresses for these people?"

"Yes." I motioned at my Rolodex.

Again Kirk nodded.

"Lieutenant Kirk," I said, "what about these inconsistencies you mentioned? I'd like to clear them up so I can get on with my work."

"What work is that?"

"Well, the press conference. And notifying our other board members so they can schedule time for a meeting."

"Taking charge rather quickly, aren't you."

It wasn't a question, so I didn't answer.

"Inconsistencies. Yes." Kirk leafed through his legal pad. "Let's see. You say the big tree of life arrived yesterday morning about eleven o'clock."

"Yes."

"And Mr. De Palma wanted it displayed for the press preview."

"Yes."

"You didn't, however."

"If you mean I didn't want it displayed, no."

"Will you go over your reasons for that again, please."

I took a breath. "The *árbol de la vida* is an ancient Mexican symbol. Some of them are quite beautiful. Most being created today, however, are a far cry from the originals. They are garish, unaesthetic. Tourists buy them, as they do those terrible paintings on velvet. They make a mockery of a sacred thing."

"And you felt this particular tree was a mockery."

"Yes."

"How is it that Mrs. Cunningham presented this mockery to the museum?"

"Isabel meant well. She liked the tree. Some people do like them, you know."

"But not you."

"Most curators would have questioned the wisdom of displaying it." What were these questions leading to?

"Then, what you're saying, Miss Oliverez, is that Mrs. Cunningham has bad taste."

"No." I closed my eyes and rubbed my forehead. "She's not an art expert, that's all. She didn't realize it would reflect badly on our collections to include such a tree. But that doesn't mean she has bad taste. If everyone were an art expert, we wouldn't need curators. We're here to select, to show the public the most definitive pieces. . . . Oh, *por Dios!*"

"What's the matter?"

"This has nothing to do with Frank's murder."

"I'll decide that, Miss Oliverez. If everyone were a crime expert, there wouldn't be policemen."

My temper flared. What right did he have to parody my statement about curators?

Kirk evidently saw the anger on my face. He smiled nastily. "You have quite a temper, don't you?"

"Only when I'm pushed."

He nodded and looked down at his paper. "All right. If this tree was such a mockery, as you put it, why would Mr. De Palma want to display it?"

"To please Isabel, of course."

"Was he fond of Mrs. Cunningham?"

"I don't understand."

"He must have been fond of her, to want to please her by displaying an ugly tree of life."

The man was baiting me, and that made me even more angry. "He was trying to please her because she has money. Surely you've heard of the influence of money, Lieutenant?"

He didn't rise to that. Instead, he made a note on his legal pad and said, "What did you tell Mr. De Palma when he said you must display the tree?"

"I told him we shouldn't."

"And?"

"He insisted, so we put it on display."

"Is that all you told him, Miss Oliverez?"

I felt a nervous tightening in my stomach. "There wasn't anything else I could tell him. He was director here."

Kirk paged through the pad. "Let me read to you from my notes on my interview with Mr. Leary: 'Frank told Elena to do it, to set the tree up. She blew her top. She has quite a temper, but I've never seen her that mad. She called Frank a son of a bitch. She told him someone ought to kill him.'" Kirk looked up. "Is that what happened, Miss Oliverez?" His mild brown eyes watched mine.

Oh, Vic! Why had he told Kirk about that? "It . . . happened," I said.

"Is that all you have to say?"

"There's nothing else *to* say. It happened. But I didn't mean it. You say things in anger, but you don't carry them out."

He made a notation on the pad. "Let's talk about the alarm system here. I take it you're familiar with it."

"Yes."

"How does it work?"

"It's a simple household system. If anyone opens any of the doors while it's on, a loud bell rings."

"What about the windows?"

"They're not on the system. Since they're all barred, it isn't necessary."

"How many doors are wired?"

"Three. The front, the loading dock, and the courtyard outside Frank's office."

Kirk frowned. "What about the doors to the central courtyard?"

"Not necessary. The only way into the courtyard is through the front door. The rear courtyard, the one outside

Frank's office, opens to the parking lot, as you've seen. The entry is protected by the padlocked gate."

"All right." He doodled on his pad. "How do you set the alarm?"

"Two ways. If you're inside, there's a toggle switch beside each door. Flipping it sets the alarm on all three doors. From the outside you have to use a key. That does the same thing—sets all three, no matter which door you use."

"And the keys? Who has them?"

"There are only two. Mine and Frank's."

"And where is yours now?"

"With me." I patted the pocket of my skirt.

"Have you had it with you all the time period we discussed, from yesterday morning to now?"

"Yes."

"And Mr. De Palma's key. Where is it, do you know?"

I paused, picturing Frank's office. "On the hook on his office wall. Frank was absentminded, so he kept both the alarm key and the key to the courtyard-gate padlock on a large ring, which he hung up when he came to work."

"You're certain there are no other keys?"

"Yes. When we moved in here there was quite a . . . discussion about who should have keys. We decided, for safety's sake, to limit the number."

"What about copies? Could any have been made?"

"No. It's not the type of key locksmiths have masters for. You have to go to the manufacturer, and they'll provide them only on the request of specified people."

"Who?"

"Which people, you mean? Me, Frank, and our board

chairman, Carlos Bautista. We would all have had to okay the request."

"And no such request has ever been made?"

"Never."

Kirk leaned back in the desk chair—*my* desk chair—and looked at me silently. "All right. Let's go over what happened when you left last night."

I sighed. "I went to Frank's office and asked if he was going to lock up or if I should do it. He told me to go ahead."

"Where were his keys then?"

"On the hook."

"And then what did you do?"

"I set the alarm and left."

"There was no one else on the premises but Mr. De Palma?"

"No one. They'd all left at least fifteen minutes before."

"So Mr. De Palma was locked in here alone?"

"Yes."

Again Kirk was silent.

"Lieutenant Kirk, I don't see why it matters what happened last night. Frank had already arrived here before I did this morning. Whoever killed him probably came in with him."

Kirk leaned forward, his imperturbab'. brown eyes on mine. "The coroner's man estimates that Mr. De Palma died early yesterday evening, possibly as early as five-thirty."

"Oh." An unpleasant realization was dawning on me. The silence lengthened.

Finally I said, "He told me he was going to work on the budget last night. But he never did that. It was Vic's job.

Maybe Frank just said that to get rid of me. Maybe he was going to meet someone here and needed to get me out of the way. Maybe he let that person in, and he or she killed him."

Kirk regarded me thoughtfully.

"Well, he *could* have let someone in," I said. "All he had to do was flip the toggle switch to shut off the alarm."

The lieutenant paged through his legal pad. "From your earlier statement, Miss Oliverez: 'When I arrived this morning, the alarm was set. Everything seemed normal. When I passed Frank's office I saw his keys on the hook and realized he'd arrived here first, but I decided not to bother him. I went about my business, and the others showed up maybe twenty minutes later.'"

"What, do you take shorthand?" I asked. But my mind was busy with the possibilities.

He didn't even acknowledge the question.

"So he let someone in last night and reset the alarm," I said. "Then that person killed him and . . ."

"And what, Miss Oliverez?"

And what indeed? No one could have left, not without the keys to reset the alarm.

"What did this person do after killing Mr. De Palma?" Kirk repeated.

"Well, he . . . he could have—" Of course! "He could have hidden in the museum until I got here this morning and then sneaked out."

"Wouldn't you or Mr. Leary or Mrs. Cunningham and her volunteers have seen someone sneak out?"

"Not necessarily . . ." I stared down at my hands. They were clasped together, white-knuckled. I closed my eyes and saw with dismaying clarity the way the alarm switch had looked when I unlocked it this morning.

"Miss Oliverez?"

I looked up at Kirk, my lips parted in panic. "Someone *did* leave the museum, though. Someone left between the time I set the alarm and the time I opened up this morning."

"How do you know that?"

"When I set the alarm last night, the lock was in the down position. But, this morning, it was up. That means someone left through one of the other two doors—the loading dock or Frank's courtyard—and reset the alarm."

"How, Miss Oliverez?"

I stared at him, thinking hard.

"How could anyone have done that when you, by your own admission, had one set of keys and the other was inside the museum when you arrived this morning?"

"Maybe—maybe someone sneaked in and replaced Frank's keys on the hook after I opened up."

"Oh, now we have someone sneaking *in*. But is that really possible, Miss Oliverez?"

"No." I'd gone straight to Frank's office and seen the keys. No one could have gotten there first.

"In other words," Kirk said, "the only person who could have set that alarm was you. We have only your word for the fact that the alarm lock was in a different position this morning—the word of a person who had, as recently as yesterday, threatened Mr. De Palma's life."

"I didn't threaten him!"

"What do you call it?"

"I—I was angry. . . . I didn't mean—"

"You appear to be an intelligent young woman, Miss

Oliverez. If you were looking at the set of facts I have before me, what would you think?"

"I . . . don't know."

"Then let me tell you." Kirk got up and leaned across the desk. His voice was soft and level. "That set of facts strongly suggests that you killed Frank De Palma."

SIX

ELEVEN O'CLOCK THAT NIGHT. I LEANED FORWARD AT MY desk, my head on my arms like a school child at rest time. The day had been grueling, and those to come seemed no more promising.

Lieutenant Kirk had kept interrogating me for two hours, going over and over my frequent quarrels with Frank and making me demonstrate how the alarm system worked. He refused to listen to my theory that Frank's killer had hidden in the museum all night and, frankly, I didn't believe it myself. All the time Kirk probed into what he referred to as my "professional jealousy of Mr. De Palma" my mind returned to that one possibility—that someone had left the museum and reset the alarm without using either set of keys. When Kirk finally let me alone, his parting warning was that I should not leave town without letting him know. I felt like a character in a TV police show.

I had then had Isabel call the press people who had been turned away that morning. At four I met with them in the central courtyard and delivered my brief statement. There was considerable grumbling about the lack of information, but they left quickly, presumably to go bother the police.

Of course, by that time my mother had heard the news. She called, full of questions and concerns. Was I all right? Did I want her to come down there?

No, Mama, I had said.

But was I sure I was all right? After all, I didn't find corpses every day, and she remembered what a terrible time I used to have at funerals.

I assured her I was all right.

That worry disposed of, my mother's voice took on confidential tones. Wasn't it awful about Frank? she asked. But hadn't she told me? Hadn't she had a feeling?

She certainly had, I replied.

Would I call her if I needed anything?

Yes, I would. I certainly would. When I hung up, there were tears in my eyes. It was wonderful in its way. No matter how old you got, your mother was still your mother.

Dinner had been bites of tasteless hamburger in between calls to our board members. Carlos Bautista's plane was due in at eight, and he would come directly to the museum for an emergency meeting. Carlos, the six other board members, and I gathered at Frank's office—which by now had been thoroughly turned upside down by the police—and, for what seemed to be the hundredth time, I went over my discovery of our director's body. The board then officially appointed me acting director, resolved that the Cinco de Mayo opening should go on as planned, and drafted a letter of condolence to the De Palma family. By the time they'd left at ten-thirty, I felt physically exhausted. I had followed the last members to the front door, thrown the toggle switch on the alarm system, and retired to my office. While my body ached for sleep, my mind kept racing.

Lieutenant Kirk had called again in the interval between the press conference and the board meeting. He wanted additional information on the museum—background information, he called it. The information, however, was more concerned with me than the museum. How long had I worked there? What was my training? Who had hired me? Did I report directly to Frank? What were my ambitions? The questions confirmed that I was indeed a serious suspect. They seemed designed more to put pressure on me than to elicit facts.

Now as I sat with my head on my desk, I considered the lieutenant. I couldn't understand how his mind worked. He seemed determined to ignore my claim that the alarm system had been set differently this morning than it had last night. It was almost as if he wanted to put the blame on me. Why? Ethnic prejudice? Some other subjective dislike of me? I couldn't tell, couldn't see what emotion, if any, hid behind those flat brown eyes. Kirk was too brown, too monochromatic. There was no telling what his reasoning might be.

Suddenly I wished I could talk this over with someone. Ideally, that person would be my sister, Carlota. We'd always been best friends; I could tell her anything. And Carlota was logical, the steady one in the family. But it was after one in the morning where she lived, in Minneapolis. I didn't want to upset her and ruin her night's sleep.

Well, I'd have to think it through myself. I hadn't been raised to be the victim of any Anglo cop. I knew I hadn't committed any murder.

Who had? I didn't know.

And how could they have? It seemed impossible.

Forget that, then, I told myself. Concentrate on Frank and your knowledge of the people around him. Almost everybody, even the Mexican Mafia members, hated him; there seemed to be no shortage of possible suspects.

I began—feeling self-conscious and a little dramatic—to review them.

Jesse. I started with him for the same reason Lieutenant Kirk had started with me. Jesse had admitted to having had a violent quarrel with Frank. What had he said? "I offered to break his fat neck." Jesse had as much of a temper as I did, if not more. But would his anger be translated into action if sufficiently pushed? I'd never had occasion to test that.

Maria. She certainly had cause to hate her uncle by marriage. Normally she rode to and from work with Frank, but yesterday she had said she was walking home. Now that I thought of it, home was farther than the delicate Maria would normally deign to walk. Where else might she have gone? I'd need to find out.

Rosa De Palma. Her husband, according to Vic, had been seeing another woman. I didn't know Rosa that well, but many women of my background accepted these affairs as part of their lot in life. Even so, didn't resentment smolder under the surface? Couldn't some event push the rejected wife over the edge? I needed to know more about Frank's widow.

The unknown woman. I needed to find out whom Frank had been seeing.

Isabel. She could have been angry at the cool reception given her *árbol de la vida*. Hadn't she said she was going to have "a few words" with Frank before leaving the museum? Had she? If so, about what?

Tony. Now I came to a real puzzle. Where the devil was the Colombian? I'd tried to call him that afternoon, but there was no answer at his apartment. Had he been so sick he couldn't answer the phone? If so, where was Susana? When Lieutenant Kirk had called late this afternoon, he'd indicated he also had had no luck when he'd gone to Tony's apartment. Kirk had merely sounded irritated about it, but to me Tony's unavailability was suspicious. Learning his whereabouts, I decided, should be my first priority.

Vic. I found it hard to suspect the big, sad man of anything. He'd been devoted to Frank. But then I thought of the look on his face when Frank had stalked out of the folk art gallery late yesterday afternoon. What did I know of Vic anyway? I would have to find out more. . . .

A sudden rasping sound raised chills along my spine and made me lift my head. The sound stopped, then started again. With a nervous laugh, I recognized the scraping of the branches of the tall jacaranda tree that draped its lavender-blue flowers over the roof of the office wing. I got up and went to the window. The fog was in, blowing in sheets across the grounds. It was so thick it might have been fine, gray snow. . . .

A shadow fell across the wall beside me. It was huge and unrecognizable and came from the doorway. I put my hand to my throat, but it did nothing to calm my racing pulse. Slowly I turned.

It was Vic.

"*Por Dios*, what are you doing here?" My voice sounded shrill and cracked.

"I'm sorry if I startled you. I didn't want to say anything to make you jump out of your skin." His homely face twisted in a grin. "I guess silence wasn't the right approach either."

"There is no right approach, not after a day like today." I hugged my jacket closer around me and came away from the window. "This place is eerie at night, especially with the fog swirling around out there."

"Come on in my office. I've got the quartz heater on. I'll give you some brandy."

It sounded good. I followed Vic across the hall. His office definitely looked cheery, the heater glowing and the curtains drawn. Ledgers and accounting sheets were spread all over the desk.

"I didn't even know you were here," I said, taking a seat in one of his comfortable old chairs. "What are you working on?"

He took a plastic cup from his desk drawer and filled it with brandy. From his high color, I guessed he'd had a fair amount of the stuff. "The accounts, what else? It occurred to me that the board would probably want to go over them, now that Frank's. . . ." He handed me the cup, his eyes melancholy. "At any rate, I wanted them to be as current as possible. With the opening coming up, I've gotten behind."

"Haven't we all." I sipped brandy, welcoming the warmth it brought.

Vic began gathering up the ledgers. "I went to your

office to make sure you didn't leave without letting me out, so you could set the alarm." He went to the small safe, twisted the dial and deposited everything inside.

"Why do you do that?" I asked.

"Do what?"

"Lock the records up. They're just papers, after all."

"They may be just papers, but they have to be kept in a fireproof place." He returned to the desk and sat, the melancholy look even more pronounced.

"You'll miss him, won't you?" I asked.

"Yes. I will. We were together a long time, almost twenty years. Frank was the closest thing to a friend I had." He must have caught my skeptical expression. "I know, you don't think Frank was capable of friendship. Well, in a lot of ways he wasn't. But we had good times. Some damned good times."

"How'd you meet him?"

"At the Hernandez Foundation." He named an organization that gave grants to Spanish-American cultural projects. "Frank was director there. It was a good job for a kid barely out of college. He hired me as his accountant. We'd travel all over the state, checking out projects we were thinking of funding. I had this old Lincoln Continental. God, could we make time in that car! San Diego to Bakersfield to San Francisco in one day. Those were some times." His eyes sobered. "Of course I needed something to keep my mind off my daughter."

It was the first time he'd ever mentioned family to me. "Why?"

"She was sick. A rare kidney disease. She . . ." He passed a hand over his eyes. "I don't want to talk about it."

That probably meant the girl had died. "When Frank left the Hernandez Foundation, you went with him?"

"Yes. Then he opened the art gallery in Old Town. He knew his art, you know. And he was good at finding sources for it. We'd bring it up from South America, Mexico. He knew who to buy from, and he could strike a hard bargain. That was before all this business about national treasures."

In recent years the governments south of the border had come to realize their art treasures are not in unlimited supply and placed restrictions on their export. In Mexico, for instance, items above five thousand dollars in value cannot be removed from the country without permission of the government. Although these restrictions originally took the form of gentlemen's agreements between countries, more and more of them are now being written into law. It was a move of which I approved, even if it did make acquisitions more difficult. "Was La Galería very successful?" I asked. I remembered it as being small but chic.

Vic nodded.

"Why'd Frank give it up, then?"

"To found this museum, of course."

That wasn't exactly how it had happened. Carlos Bautista and several of his wealthy cronies had come up with the idea and hired Frank to implement it. He, in turn, had hired me. "I always pictured Frank as very fond of money, and we all know he wasn't making that much here. I'm surprised he would give up a lucrative business."

Vic waved one hand. "That was one of the stipulations that went with the job, so there wouldn't be a conflict of interest. And there was the prestige of the directorship.

Frank never could resist a chance to better his standing in the community."

Was there a touch of bitterness in Vic's voice?

"Also," he added, "he'd invested his profits from La Galería wisely. He really didn't need a big salary."

I supposed it made sense. If anyone would be privy to the workings of Frank's mind, it would be Vic.

"This morning," I said, "you mentioned that Frank was involved with a woman other than Rosa."

Vic shook his head. "I shouldn't have told you."

"Who is she?"

"I'm sorry. I can't say."

"Vic, it might be important."

He looked surprised. "To what?"

"To finding out who killed him."

"Oh, no. I don't think so."

"Won't you tell me?"

"Elena, there are some things I can't talk about."

I was silent for a moment. "They suspect me, you know."

"That's silly. You wouldn't kill anyone."

"But you told them what I said to Frank, that someone ought to kill him. Why did you do that, Vic?"

"Elena, I'm sorry. But I thought it would be better not to cover it up. I mean, someone would have told, and they might not have put it in so favorable a light."

I didn't consider his mention of it especially favorable, but I held my tongue. "Now that I've been named acting director, it looks even worse to the police."

"Nonsense. You were the logical choice for the job. And don't worry about the police; they'll find the real killer, and then we can get on with our business. What do you bet they offer you the director's job?"

I shrugged. Right now, it didn't really matter.

"Don't look down your nose at it. It's a plum for someone your age."

"Maybe." I was thinking about my new duties and all the things I had to do before the opening. I would need to rely heavily on Vic in the next few days. Perhaps he should have Frank's keys to the museum. But something kept me from mentioning it. For now, I'd keep both sets.

I stood up, yawning. "I'd better be getting home. And you should, too. We've got a busy day tomorrow."

Vic stood up. He got his jacket and followed me out. The mist was still sheeting across the lawn. I set the alarm, and Vic and I walked through the fog to our cars.

SEVEN

I DIDN'T GO HOME, OF COURSE. INSTEAD I DROVE ACROSS town to the district near Santa Barbara City College, where Tony lived. It wasn't exactly a rundown area, but it was filled with fast-food stands, health food stores, and other businesses catering to students. Even at this hour and in this fog, young people wandered along the sidewalks and congregated on street corners. It hadn't been so many years since I'd been a student myself, but now I felt out of place among so many fresh faces. I wondered why Tony had chosen to live here, then remembered Susana was in her first year at the college.

Tony's street was all apartments, complex after complex, all of them with floodlit facades and pretentious names. Tony's was called the Lanai, a stucco building with a Hawaiian motif, built around a central court with a swimming pool. A chandelier shaped liked the head of a tiki god hung on a chain in the arched entryway. In the courtyard the imitation Hawaiian torchlights were dimmed by the mist. I stood by the pool, studying the second tier of apartments where Tony lived. They were all dark except the middle one. I moved closer and spotted the number—207. It was Tony's.

Half-past midnight was not a good time to go calling. But, then, Tony had been unavailable all day. I could say I needed to talk to him about the situation at the museum. And the lateness of the hour might catch him off guard. I started for the wrought iron stairway, then paused when I heard car doors slam and footsteps coming from the street.

Tony's voice said in Spanish, "Home at last." I ducked under the stairs, into the foliage of a large fuschia bush.

Tony and Susana came through the archway and crossed the courtyard. He carried a suitcase, and his thin shoulders slumped as if he were exhausted. Susana walked along in her usual bouncy gait, snapping her gum. They climbed the stairs, and moments later I heard the apartment door slam.

I remained under the stairs, fuschia blossoms tickling my cheek. Where on earth had Tony been? And for how long? When had I seen him last?

I thought back to the afternoon before. Yes, he'd been there when we'd set the tree of life in place around five o'clock. That would have given him less than thirty-two hours to go—where?

And what should I do? I could rush up there and demand to know where he'd been. Probably, though, he wouldn't let me in at this time of night. And if he did, he wasn't likely to tell me what was going on, since he'd gone to some length to hide it already. If it had something to do with

Frank's murder, the situation could turn ugly, even dangerous.

Could Tony have been in the museum when I left last night? Quarreled with Frank and killed him? Then somehow managed to slip out? He might have come home, packed a bag and run. But if he was on the run, why had he returned? No, Tony had gone away for another reason, something Susana's call about his alleged illness had been designed to cover up. I thought of all those other calls in the last six months. They came at three- to four-week intervals, and Tony was usually sick for five or more days. Maybe Tony had been away on mysterious business each time. That was a lot of traveling.

I slipped out from under the stairs and looked up at the apartment. The living room lights, behind closed draperies, were still on. I'd been to Tony's place only once, at Christmas time, for one of those awful parties for business associates that everyone wishes the host didn't feel obligated to throw. Thinking back on that party, I pictured the layout of the apartment.

The living room ran the full length of it and opened on the other side to a balcony overlooking the parking lot— one of those design idiocies that contemporary California builders were always committing. The kitchen was also at the rear, and had access to the parking lot by a stairway. I hurried out of the courtyard to the street.

There at the curb was Susana's little Triumph. I went up and felt the hood. The engine was hot. Tony's car would probably be parked in the stall that went with the apartment. I walked down the driveway toward it and located his new Mustang. The engine was cold; it must have been sitting there all day.

The curtains of the apartment's kitchen were drawn, but

light shone through them. I crept up the stairs to the little service porch. The window was open slightly and I could hear Tony's and Susana's voices. They were talking in the clipped accents of South American Spanish, made harsher by anger. I moved closer and peered through the place where the curtains didn't quite meet.

Tony stood at the counter, pouring what looked like whiskey into a glass. Susana was in the center of the kitchen, her arms folded, one foot tapping on the floor. She tossed her mane of teased black hair and said, "What do you mean, you're giving it up?"

"Just what I said. I am not going to do it again."

"But, now that Frank is dead, it will be all yours."

"Mine and Robert's and Vic's."

She dismissed the others with an imperious wave of her hand. "But mainly yours."

I was surprised. This was not the giggly sixteen-year-old Susana I knew.

"That doesn't matter. I told you, I am through."

Now Susana reverted to type, her lower lip pushing out in a pout. "But the money! Where will we get the money for all the pretty things?"

Tony sipped from his glass and set it down on the counter. "Don't worry about money, my love. Now I will become director. The job pays much more than education director."

"But as director, you could carry on your other business easily."

His face darkened. "Enough! I hate those trips. I have decided."

"You won't get the job anyway," Susana said spitefully. "Not with that Elena around. She'll see that you don't get it. She wants it herself." She spoke my name with a venom that took me aback.

Tony went up and put his arm around Susana. "Don't worry about Elena, either. She is no problem."

"So there will still be money?" She looked up at him with wide, childlike eyes.

Tony caressed her cheek. "Yes, money and pretty things. Whatever you want."

"Money for a television for the bedroom? And maybe a week in Hawaii?"

"Yes, love."

"Maui. That is where all the beautiful people go. We will go to Maui."

"Yes, love." His hand moved down her throat toward one of her full breasts.

This I didn't need to witness. I turned away.

The distance between the service porch and the balcony off the living room was only a few feet. I went over to the iron railing and looked down at the ground. It wasn't much of a drop, so I climbed onto the railing, deciding to chance it. For a moment, my foot on the other railing, my hands clammy as I reached to pull myself across, I faltered. Then I closed my eyes, pulled, and landed on the balcony, stumbling. They hadn't bothered to close the living room draperies on this side.

The room was decorated in stark, modern furniture, all chrome and glass and light wood. After the discussion I had just heard about Tony's "other business," I looked at the furniture with interest. Expensive. It had to have cost thousands of dollars for this room alone. There was an elaborate stereo set in a teak cabinet, a large TV with a video recorder, and what looked like original artworks on glass-enclosed shelves. It was not the living room of the education director of a small, impecunious museum.

One of the lights that had been left on was by the door to the bedrooms. Tony's suitcase sat on the floor. I went forward, skirting a kettle-style barbecue and a lawn chair, and pressed my face to the glass. The suitcase had a yellow tag that said LAX, the code letters for Los Angeles International Airport. Unfortunately, that didn't help me figure out where Tony had been. There was also another tag, a blue one with a symbol on it. I strained my eyes, but all I could tell was that it looked like a compass, one with all the points, not just north, south, east, and west.

The light in the kitchen went out. Tony and Susana appeared in the door to the living room. I jerked back from the glass and banged into the barbecue. It made a hollow sound, like a bell ringing.

"What was that?" Tony started for the balcony door.

I looked around frantically. There was a pile of fireplace wood in one corner. I leaped for it and squeezed behind, a piece of bark scraping my skin. The balcony light came on as I crouched there, holding my breath.

The glass door slid open, and footsteps sounded on the concrete floor. After a moment Tony said, "Huh."

"What is it?" Susana asked.

"I don't see anything."

"Probably it was a cat. They are always jumping over from the neighbors' balcony."

"Probably. I ought to speak to the manager. They don't allow cats in this building."

"But it is a nice cat. I am thinking of getting one myself."

"No cats, my love," Tony said firmly. His footsteps went

inside, the balcony light went out, and the door slammed shut.

I let out my breath slowly. There was no way I could have explained my presence on Tony's balcony at one in the morning. And the scene would have quickly turned ugly had they realized I'd overheard them talking. I was going to have to be more cautious in the future.

After five minutes, when the light in the living room had gone out, I climbed back over to the service porch and hurried away from there to my car. As I drove home through the thick mist, my mind whirled with the possibilities.

Tony, Vic, Fran, and his brother Robert had had another business. Susana had said it would be all Tony's now that Frank was dead, which meant Frank had been much more important in the scheme than either Vic or Robert. The scheme obviously involved travel on Tony's part. Travel for what? And where to?

Well, I had one clue.

I pulled into my driveway and rushed into the house. The day's heat was still trapped there, and it felt warm after the fog. I turned on the living room lights and went to my desk. My hands were shaking with excitement as I pulled the Yellow Pages from the drawer.

Airlines. Or was it listed as air lines, two words? I never remembered and always looked up the wrong spelling first. Airlines. No. Air lines.

I hoped that whatever carrier Tony had flown was large enough to have an ad showing its symbol. I started at the beginning, with Aer Lingus. There were plenty of symbols—stylized initials, wings, geese, ducks, and kiwi birds. No compass, however. TWA, Transamerica, UTA, United. Still no compass. I turned the page, and there it was, right at the top. Varig Brasilian Airlines. "Jets from U.S.A. to South America, Africa, and Japan."

That covered a lot of territory, but I was willing to bet on South America, possibly Bogotá, where Tony was from. Varig flew out of L.A. International, and Tony's bag had been coded for a return trip there. This called for mathematics, never my strong suit. I took out a pencil and a piece of scratch paper.

I wrote, "12:30," the approximate time Tony had returned home, near the bottom of the page. How long did it take to drive here from L.A. International? At this time of night, in light traffic, about two hours. Farther up the page, I wrote, "10:30."

All right. I'd have to knock off another hour for baggage claim and customs. I crossed out the other figure and wrote "9:30."

That was it: I wanted a Varig flight arriving at LAX at around nine-thirty. Varig had a twenty-four-hour information and reservations line. I pulled the phone toward me and dialed.

When the sleepy-sounding clerk answered, I said, "I'm interested in service from Bogotá. I understand you have a flight that arrives around nine-thirty in the evening."

"Service to or from Bogotá?"

"From."

"Just a moment, please." There were background noises that sounded as if he was typing. "I'm sorry, our flight from Bogotá gets in at seven-oh-five."

"Are you sure? I mean, I thought there was a flight around nine-thirty."

"No, the computer says seven-oh-five, ma'am."

"Well, what *does* get in at around nine-thirty?"

"You wanted service from Bogotá. . . . "

"Could you check and see where the nine-thirty flight originates? I'd sleep better knowing."

Surprisingly, he laughed. "I get what you mean. Hold on." The typing noises began again. "You're talking about our flight from Rio. It arrives at nine-forty-seven."

"Rio?" I'd been to Rio; it was more than a thirteen-hour flight. Tony could not possibly have gone there and back, plus cleared customs and traveled to and from the airport, in the time allotted. "Does it stop anywhere?"

"Yes, Lima, Peru."

"Lima. How long a flight is that?"

"About seven hours."

Tony could have done that easily. "What about the flight to Lima? When does that leave?"

"Ten-thirty-eight in the evening."

"Thanks," I said, "you've been a great help."

"Do you want to book any of those flights?"

"Um, no. I've got to think about it."

"Fine. And will you be able to sleep better—knowing about the Rio flight?"

"I certainly will."

"Sweet dreams." He probably thought I was one of those lonely people who make phone calls to airlines in the middle of the night so they can hear another human voice.

I'd asked about service from Bogotá on the off chance Tony had been called home on some family emergency. But instead he'd been to Lima, Peru—however briefly. Now I could reconstruct the scenario of what had happened.

Tony had returned home some time after five yesterday, and Susana had driven him to L.A. International. The latest he could have left Santa Barbara in order to make the flight was seven-thirty. That still gave him plenty of time to kill Frank. Of course, I had my doubts Tony was smart enough to figure a way out of the museum that neither the police nor I could understand, but I'd worry about that later.

Okay, Tony had flown to Lima and probably been asleep in his hotel or wherever he was staying by the time Susana had called him to say Frank was dead—or that his body had been discovered. Since his absence would have looked suspicious, he'd caught the return flight, and Susana had covered for him all day by not answering the phone or door.

But, if he'd killed Frank, would he have returned? Maybe, if he thought he wouldn't be suspected.

But then, why fly to Lima at all? Did Tony take these trips every time he called in sick? Were they always to Lima, or did he travel to other cities? And why?

Whatever the reason, I had a feeling it wasn't legal.

EIGHT

THE NEXT MORNING THE PAPER WAS FULL OF NEWS ABOUT Frank's murder. The coverage was factual, but there was an undertone of questions. Why had this happened practically on the eve of the museum's opening? What had the director been doing alone in the galleries after the museum had closed its doors for the day? Was one of the other employees a possible suspect? Could the director somehow have brought this on himself?

I wondered if the questions would have been so thinly veiled had we not been a minority museum. And I also wondered what more publicity of this type would do to us.

As official representative of the museum, I had to pay a condolence call on the De Palmas. I puttered around the house until nearly eleven, then got into the car and drove north through town. Frank's family lived in a sprawling single-story ranch house on one of the streets that wound high on a bluff above Santa Barbara Point. It wasn't Montecito, where Isabel lived in lonely splendor in her Spanish-style mansion, but it was not bad for a boy who had come out of the barrio. Twenty years ago, real estate agents would have steered anyone with a surname like De Palma away from this district. Times had changed, however, and Frank's neighbors were glad to have a citizen of the chic art world right across the fence. I doubted they invited the De Palmas to their parties, though.

Frank's brother Robert answered the door. His face was dour and jowly, and his hair hung down in greasy-looking strands. His dark suit fit him like a sausage casing. Still, I looked at him with new interest. This was not merely rotund Robert; it was the man who had illicit dealings with his brother, Vic, and Tony. Robert looked back blearily and motioned me into the living room.

It was a large room filled with overstuffed furniture. On the walls were abstract paintings by several of our better-known contemporary painters. I looked at them, as I had at Robert, with renewed interest. Granted, Frank had owned a gallery and had known how to strike bargains, but the paintings could not have been cheap in any case.

Rosa De Palma and Maria were seated on the sectional sofa, both dressed in black. Rosa's plump but still handsome face was puffed from crying. Maria waved at me, almost gaily, and I caught Robert frowning at her. Rosa made a moaning sound and stood. She rushed across the room and threw her arms around me, sobbing. I patted her on the back and whispered ineffectual expressions of sympathy. It reminded me of the emotional funerals of my childhood, where relatives had howled out their grief—and then come back to our house to stuff themselves at my mother's buffet two hours later.

Maria made an impatient noise and came over to us. She extricated me from Rosa's embrace and led her aunt back to the couch. As Rosa sat, Jesse entered through an archway at the rear of the room. He carried a tray with a coffee pot and cups. I stared at him.

Jesse grinned sheepishly and set the tray on the coffee table. "Yeah, they're domesticating me."

Rosa blew her nose. "Maria should have done that."

"Maria does too much."

"Work is good for the girl."

Jesse shrugged and began pouring coffee. I sat down on a hassock and accepted a cup. Robert remained over by the fireplace, one elbow on the mantel. When Jesse offered him coffee, he declined by shaking his head.

"So, Elena," Rosa said, "you are taking over for Frank."

"I am acting director, yes."

"It is good of you. The museum must go on. It was my husband's dream, his *inspiració.*"

Por Dios, could the woman really believe that? She was painting her hypocritical little husband as some sort of visionary. I glanced at Jesse, who was studiously staring into his coffee cup. From Maria came the faintest of snorts. Even Robert shifted uneasily from one foot to the other. When I looked back at Rosa, her eyes met mine. They were hard, daring me or anyone else to contradict her.

She knows, I thought. She knows what he was; but she'll never admit it. Rosa De Palma was made of the stuff that kept Chicano families together, that maintained pride and dignity against all odds. I had to admire—and pity—her.

I turned to Jesse. "I hate to talk business at a time like

this, but we'll need you at the museum today. We want you to set up an additional display of *camaleones*."

"Ah, of course." I'd been afraid he would ask where and, for obvious reasons, I didn't want to bring up the folk art gallery. But the *árbol de la vida* had been destroyed, and something had to take its place before the opening. I had decided we might as well promote Jesse and his colorful animals.

"Can you get to it today?" I asked.

He nodded. "I have a few *camaleones* at my studio that will complement those that are already on display. Perhaps I should get started right away?" He looked relieved to have an excuse to leave the De Palma house.

"Yes, if you would. In case there are any problems, you know."

Jesse stood. He took Rosa's hand. She squeezed his and thanked him effusively for all he'd done. Maria got up and accompanied him to the door. As they passed Robert, he nodded curtly at Jesse. The couple went outside and half-closed the door behind them.

Robert left his post at the fireplace and went to sit beside Rosa. His eyes were narrowed. "About time the young punk left," he muttered.

Rosa patted his hand. "It's all right, Roberto. She'll get over him. It is only an *infatuación*."

He grunted.

I said, "I take it you're not too fond of Jesse."

Rosa shook her head. "He's a nice enough boy, but he is not right for Maria. A flighty girl like that needs someone older, more stable." Again she patted Robert's hand.

Robert glared at her. "How can you say he's nice enough, after what he did to my brother?"

"Hush."

Jesse had done something to Frank? "What happened?"

They exchanged looks. "Ah, well, that's in the past," Rosa said.

"Past," Robert said, "but not forgotten. The punk got in a fight with him. Knocked him around pretty bad. Gave him a black eye. That's not something you forget so easy."

"*Dios mio!* When was this?"

"A couple of months ago. Right before Frank's vacation. He took off early so he didn't have to go to work and explain it."

I remembered Frank calling in sick the Friday before his vacation was due to start. At the time I'd thought it a ploy so the family could leave early for Baja California. This shed new light on his absence and, unfortunately, on Jesse's relations with our director. Jesse had admitted to quarrels—but a fist fight? Again I thought of the artist's quick temper. How many quarrels would it have taken to push him over the edge?

Maria entered and slammed the door. She came halfway across the room and stopped, her eyes flashing. "I heard what you were saying about Jesse."

Rosa sighed. "Maria, Roberto was only telling what happened."

"He had no right! Why does she"—she gestured at me—"have to know?"

"What does it matter?"

"It makes my fiancé look bad."

Robert sucked in his breath and began to cough.

"Since when," Rosa said, "is he your fiancé"

"Since yesterday. My uncle is gone. He cannot stop me from marrying now."

Rosa's face reddened. "Have you no respect? Don't you honor the memory of your uncle?"

"Why should I? Did he have respect for me, for my love for Jesse?"

Robert half rose, but Rosa pulled him back down. "Maria," she said evenly, "the children need you."

"The children! They always need something."

"Maria, go see how they are."

"I am sick and tired of—"

"Go!" The anger in Rosa's eyes would have sent me running from the room. Maria, however, merely glared at her and ambled insolently through the archway toward the rear of the house. A door slammed back there, and Rosa burst into tears.

Now it was Robert's turn to pat Rosa's hand. I shifted uncomfortably on the hassock, glancing at my watch and thinking of an excuse to go. Maria's display of defiance surprised me; while Frank was alive, she had been sulky and resentful, but had confined her rebellion to snippy asides and glares when he wasn't looking. His death had unleashed a pent-up fury.

Or had the unleashing of that fury, for whatever reason, caused his death?

"She is ungrateful," Robert said to Rosa.

Rosa sighed. "Perhaps we have been too hard on her."

"That kind of girl you have to be hard on. You took her in, didn't you? You gave her a chance to make up for her mistakes. And now look how she rewards you."

Her mistakes? I remained silent.

"Perhaps if she'd stayed in Mazatlán," Rosa said, "If she'd married the boy, had her baby. . . ."

"The boy didn't want to marry her. He claimed anyone could have been the father—and Maria admitted that."

"But to go off and have an abortion!" Rosa crossed herself. "When my sister found out, it almost killed her."

Suddenly Robert glanced at me; they had been talking as if, for the moment, they'd forgotten I was there. "That's over and done," he said firmly. "She came to you and did well in her secretarial course. She has a good job. When she gets over this Jesse nonsense she'll be fine. In the meantime, she's probably just upset over Frank's death, like the rest of us." His eyes were on me the whole time he spoke.

I said, "Yes, Rosa. You have to realize Maria is very young. We all make mistakes at her age. Why, I remember . . ." I stopped. I couldn't think of anything I had done that was major—or that I wanted to air in the De Palma living room.

I stood up, embraced Rosa and went to the door. "Don't worry about the museum, Rosa. The opening will come off exactly as Frank would have wanted. And when you know about the funeral arrangements, please have someone call us."

Rosa nodded absently. Robert stood and followed me out. On the front walk, he stopped me, his hand on my shoulder. "You won't repeat what you heard here, Elena?"

"Of course not." Not unless it became important in the murder investigation. I slipped out of Robert's grasp and hurried to my car.

Maria was no angel, I reflected as I drove to the museum. But just because a good Catholic girl messes around with every boy in town and then has an abortion, it doesn't mean she's capable of murdering her uncle. Not necessarily, anyway.

At any rate, the morning had been enlightening.

When I arrived at the museum Isabel was sitting at Maria's desk, reading an art dealer's catalog. She looked up as I came in, her eyes ringed with dark circles. In spite of her obvious fatigue, her hair and white tennis dress were as tidy as ever.

"That Lieutenant Kirk called you, Elena."

"Oh? What does he want?"

"To see you. He said he would be out for a few hours, but that you're to come to his office at four this afternoon."

"Demanding, isn't he?" I tried to make light of it, but a hunted feeling settled over me. My tone didn't fool Isabel either. She gave me a sympathetic nod and returned to her catalog.

I looked around the outer office. Through the open door of his cubicle I spotted Tony, sitting with his feet on his desk, his head haloed by clouds of cigarette smoke. This was what wanted to become director of the museum! Well, that certainly wouldn't happen—not after I found out the purpose of his secret trips to South America. I reached for the Rolodex on Maria's desk and turned it until I found the card for the travel agency the museum used. I pulled it off the wheel and took it to my office, shutting the door behind me.

The person who answered the phone at the travel agency passed my call along to a Mrs. DeLano, the representative we dealt with. I explained that I was trying to find out which of Mr. Ibarra's tickets to South America had been paid for and which were outstanding. Mrs. DeLano went to get her file.

"Your statement is up to date, Miss Oliverez. Seven first class tickets to various South American destinations. We certainly appreciate the business."

First class! "Mrs. DeLano, can you give me the number of the museum checks the last two tickets were paid for with?"

"Yes. Just a minute." She rustled through some papers and then read off two sets of digits to me.

"Do you recall if those were both signed by Mr. Leary?"

"I believe so. They usually are." She paused. "Is there some problem?"

"Nothing that should concern you. Our files are a bit disordered, what with moving and all."

"Of course. By the way, we were very sorry to hear about Mr. De Palma. Will you still be holding your opening?"

"Yes, we will." I thanked her for her help and hung up, feeling sad. So they'd all been in on it, whatever it was—Frank, Tony, Robert, and Vic. It was Vic's involvement that I didn't want to believe. Vic, the gentle, unhappy man who had treated me like a daughter. I remembered our talk last night and my—at the time—strange reluctance to trust him with the other set of museum keys. That reluctance proved to have been well founded.

What was I going to do about this? I wondered. I could go to the police. But first I should go to Carlos Bautista. Carlos had a bad temper, though, and this was sure to set it off. By the time he was through, the mess would be spread all over the papers. And a scandal so soon after Frank's murder would ruin us.

What was I going to do?

Ordinarily I would have thought my colleagues stupid for using the museum's travel agent and checks to finance whatever they were doing in South America. But since they'd all been in on it—possibly even Maria—they'd been reasonably safe in doing so. The board examined the accounts once a year. I never looked at them, didn't understand them. And the ledgers were kept in the safe, away from prying eyes; I'd seen Vic lock them up only last night. Probably he'd been working late doctoring the books; he knew they'd come under scrutiny now that Frank was dead.

If Frank hadn't been murdered while Tony was off in Peru, I probably would never have caught on to anything. And neither would the board, because Vic would have fixed all discrepancies.

My mind returned to the matter of the extra keys. Until everything was cleared up, they should be kept in a safe place. I went to Frank's office. The keys were still there, on their hook. I took them down, brushing at a dirt smudge on the wall with my other hand. We'd been in this building less than a month, and already it was going to seed. Was it merely a reflection of the pettiness and dishonesty of the building's occupants? I wondered.

Enough of this brooding, Elena, I thought sternly. It was time to see how Jesse was doing in the folk art gallery.

He was stringing wire from which to hang a *camaleón*. And Vic, the last person I wanted to see, was with him. When they turned, I avoided Vic's eyes; then, feeling his on me, I looked back at him. His face was more haggard than Isabel's, his clothes rumpled, and his cardigan sweater buttoned wrong. Like the building, the staff was going to pieces.

Vic apparently didn't want to see me either. He quickly excused himself, mumbling something about paying some bills. I turned to Jesse.

He lifted a brightly colored *camaleón* and fastened it to the wire. This one was a sort of Pegasus. Its wings caught the breeze from the ventilation system, and it began to turn as soon as Jesse stepped back. As usual, his eyes held reverence, and suddenly it sickened me. Did he think he was that great an artist? The *camaleones* were beautiful, but they didn't make him a Picasso.

Jesse saw my expression, which must have been quite sour. "What's wrong?"

I shrugged. Why not get it over with? "I heard some nasty talk at the De Palmas' after you left."

"Oh, yeah?"

"Yes. About you. And about Maria."

"You mean that we're engaged? An engagement isn't exactly what I'd call nasty."

"Not about your engagement, although that came up, too. Let's talk about the time you gave Frank the black eye."

His face closed up, and he turned back to the *camaleón*. "Who brought that up?"

"Robert."

"He would. He wants to marry Maria, you know."

"That's not the point, Jesse. What counts is that your fights with Frank were much more serious than you let on."

"So?"

"So, if you hit a person once, you might—"

He whirled on me, his shoe-button eyes flat with anger. "Are you trying to say I killed Frank?"

"I'm trying to say how it will look to the police."

"And how are they going to find out?"

"I did. It's likely they will, too."

"Especially if you tell them."

"Did I say I would?"

"You didn't have to. They suspect you, and you'll do anything to save your own neck."

Well, of course I would. "Then there's the matter of Maria's rather checkered past. Did you know about that?"

"We have no secrets from one another. Okay, she was wild. She's the oldest in a big family. All the others are boys. Her parents ignored her. She wanted some attention."

"She certainly got it."

"Look, Elena, why are you coming off so holier-than-thou? You're not exactly the Virgin Mary yourself. So Maria made a mistake. But if you're trying to say she had something to do with Frank's death, forget it. An abortion isn't murder."

"Some would say it is."

The words hung heavily in the quiet room. Jesse and I stared at each other. We were both educated, liberal-minded, and free. I didn't go to church much anymore. I assumed he didn't either. But weren't there vestiges of our strict Catholic upbringing buried deep in our subconscious minds? Apparently so, from this sudden silence.

I didn't want to argue with him anymore. This wasn't getting us anywhere. I turned abruptly and left the gallery.

Inwardly I was seething. My teeth were clenched so tightly that my gums ached. My fists were balled, finger-nails digging into my palms. This kind of tension wasn't going to help me—either in bringing off the Cinco de

Mayo party or in clearing myself of Frank's murder. I decided to work it off by going to the cellar and performing some housekeeping tasks.

A museum conservator—and here I was both curator and preserver of our collections—performs many of these chores. They are boring, routine, delicate, and about as much fun as scrubbing the bathroom floor. But there is always a kind of soothing quality to them. When I am removing minute dust particles from a statue or inspecting an old church manuscript for mold, time slows down for me, and I can let my mind rest or wander where it pleases. This was the sort of natural tranquilizer I needed now.

Unfortunately, before I could even get at our artifacts, I would have to perform the duties of a stevedore. Everything was all heaped together, a jumble of cartons and fixtures and even office furniture. The ruins of the *árbol de la vida* leaned at a crazy angle in the middle of the room. Someone had left a flashlight on a crate near the stairs, and I took it to the front, figuring I'd start in the farthest corner. At least the shelves were clear and clean up there. I could unpack some of the boxes, see where things were.

I had packed only those items in our collections we had planned to display for the opening. A generous donation from a board member had allowed us to hire the moving company that had transported the King Tut exhibit for the rest. The real problem now was that I wasn't exactly sure how they'd packed things or where those boxes were. I set the flashlight on a shelf so it provided maximum light, then ripped the tape from the top of the nearest carton.

These were our Olmec jadeite figurines. Good. After the opening, when I shifted the pre-Hispanic displays, they'd look good in the large showcase. I placed the figurines—a cross between humans and jaguars, a prevalent theme in that pre-Christian Indian civilization—carefully on the shelf.

The next box wasn't one of the moving company's, and I didn't recognize it. That didn't surprise me. We were a small museum, but even for us packing had taken many days and become disorganized. I reached in and unwrapped a statue of the Aztec earth goddess Coatlicue.

And stared at it. Turned it over in my hands. Felt it wonderingly.

This statue was not from our collections. I had never seen it before.

Quickly I set it on the shelf and fumbled with the next felt-wrapped shape. It was another Aztec statue, of Xochipilli, god of flowers and music. He looked at me through the paradoxical death mask the deity always wears. The statue was beautiful, valuable, and totally unfamiliar to me.

I began pawing through the other boxes. There were pre-Hispanic figurines, colonial religious paintings, Spanish crosses, and Peruvian gold work. There were silver *milagros*—votive offerings—like those in my own collection. There were funerary urns, dance masks, and fertility symbols.

I had never seen any of them before in my life.

NINE

I SAT DOWN ON A CRATE AND SURVEYED WHAT I'D FOUND. Some, like the silver *milagros*, were from Mexico, but most were from South America. South America, where Tony frequently traveled using museum funds.

Had he smuggled all these artifacts into the United States? No, there would be no need to; most of them didn't fall into the category of national treasures. Those that did were of the sort that could be sold to a museum, and Tony could prove he was our representative. This cache of artifacts had probably been legitimately purchased—again, I was sure, with museum funds.

The only problem was that *I* was the one who was supposed to make such acquisitions.

I had struggled to make do with our existing collections. I had spent hours developing innovative and pleasing arrangements for the same old displays. I often dreamed at

night of acquiring some really good reform period land-
scapes. And, in the meantime, Tony had been flying first
class to South America on buying trips. Not trips to build
up the museum's collections, however. I knew these artifacts were not intended to appear in our galleries.

I remembered the sheet of ledger paper I'd found in
Frank's desk the day of his murder—the one with the list
of names and amounts. Those amounts roughly matched
the value I would place on certain of these artifacts, or
groups of them. The names were probably those of their
buyers. As I sat there, their scheme became clearer and I
felt the stirrings of rage.

While the museum foundered, lacking money to print
decent catalogs, to hire a security guard, or even to pay the
light bill, its director, business manager, and education
director had siphoned off badly needed funds into their
own money-making scheme. Frank, with his buying ex-
pertise, had located sources for artworks. Of course, he
couldn't be gone too often; ineffective as he was, his presence was necessary if he was to keep his job. So he sent
Tony, an employee so useless he would hardly be missed,
off to South America. Bubble-headed Susana covered for
him; no one would suspect anyone that silly of trickery.
And Vic—he signed the checks. What about Robert? Probably just along for the ride, cashing in on his brother's
cleverness.

It would be easy for Frank to find buyers for their wares.
He'd operated a gallery for a long time. He knew all the
local collectors. He might even be using La Galería as a
front, letting the new owner sell the stuff and keep a com-
mission. Who was the new owner, anyway? I dimly

recalled that Frank had sold out to a woman newly arrived from Los Angeles. Or had he sold at all?

It was my business to find out now. No one was going to destroy my museum for his own profit.

But how did this connect with Frank's murder? Had one of the thieving *bastardos* had a falling out with him? If so—Tony? He seemed too stupid to pull it off, but maybe the stupidity, like Susana's silliness, was only an act. Vic? Hard to believe, but I was learning more about Vic every day. Robert? Even harder; he was Frank's brother. But, then, brother had been killing brother since the beginning of time.

And, of course, there was the big question: what to do about these artifacts? If I had thought I had a potentially ruinous situation on my hands an hour ago, it was infinitely worse now.

I stood up and began repacking the boxes. No one must know I'd found them. Not yet, at any rate. When I was done, I grabbed the flashlight, returned it to where it had been, and went upstairs. In my office I sat down to think, then got up and paced. I clasped my hands together, almost wringing them, and muttered aloud in Spanish, "What can I do? What *am* I going to do?"

"Elena?" It was Isabel's voice, tentative and alarmed. She stood in the doorway, frowning. "Elena, are you all right?"

"No. No, I am not all right."

She came inside, shutting the door. "Can I help in any way?"

"No one can help."

"Is it that lieutenant? You're afraid he thinks you killed

Frank? But you shouldn't worry. We all know you couldn't have done it."

I stared at her. I had actually forgotten Dave Kirk for a time.

Isabel's frown deepened. "Elena, what *is* it?"

I took a deep breath. "Sit down. I've got something to tell you."

She sat. I continued pacing and told her the whole story. As I spoke, her already sallow face went paler.

"I was afraid of something like that," she said. "I've never trusted Frank. Why do you think I spend so much time here? I've watched him so carefully—and yet I didn't see."

"It never even occurred to me to watch him. And now that I've found out, no matter what I do, there will be a nasty scandal. People may even think we were all in on it, that the museum is nothing more than a front. The papers will put racial overtones on it."

Isabel nodded.

"But I can't just let them get away with it."

"No." Her eyes hardened.

"If I go to Carlos now, he'll drag it all out into the open. And a scandal before the Cinco de Mayo party is sure to ruin the museum. People will demand refunds on their tickets. The others who might show up at the door won't. We'll lose all our support."

"I don't think you should tell anyone yet," Isabel said. "After the opening, that's different."

"It'll still be a scandal."

"Yes, but we will have collected fifty dollars a head from each person attending the Cinco de Mayo party." Her eyes took on a hawklike fundraiser's gleam. "We need that money. Afterward, go to Carlos. Perhaps you can convince him to be discreet."

I didn't like it. I couldn't see how I could go on until the opening, working beside those people, knowing what I did. But it made sense.

"It's not likely they will remove the artifacts from the cellar before the opening," Isabel went on. "There are too many people around. So you know the evidence will remain safe."

"They could do it at night."

"Did you give keys to the building to any of them?"

"No. I have both sets."

"There, you see?"

"I suppose you're right."

"Of course I'm right. Somehow we will see this through. The museum will not suffer."

Isabel's face was earnest and drawn. Suddenly I had one of those odd sensations you get, as if you're looking at a person you've never seen before, rather than a familiar friend. I said, "Isabel, what happened when you had your 'few words' with Frank the day he was killed?"

She started. "What words?"

"You said you were going to talk to him about something."

"Oh, that. I only wanted to . . . to warn him about his appearance at the press preview. Frank could be so sloppy, you know."

"And did you?"

"No. I . . . I couldn't find him."

"He was in the courtyard, with his plants."

"Oh?"

"I told you he might be."

"I guess I didn't look."

I watched her, saying nothing.

"Elena, what are you implying?" Isabel's hand went to her throat.

"I was just curious."

Isabel's eyes widened. "Elena, you don't think I killed Frank?"

"Somebody did. And it was probably somebody connected with the museum."

"But *me*?" Her hand remained where it was, clutching at the neck of her tennis dress.

Suddenly I felt ashamed. "I'm sorry, Isabel. I shouldn't go around accusing people. But I don't know what to think anymore. Look at Vic. He was one of my favorite people, and now my faith in him has been totally destroyed. After that, I can truthfully say that anybody could have killed Frank—Vic, you, Robert, Maria, Jesse, Tony, even Susana."

"Susana?" Now Isabel looked truly shocked.

"She was in on the embezzlement, too."

"But—Susana?"

I shrugged.

"I don't think you should be speculating like this," Isabel said.

"Why not?"

"It's dangerous." She shivered. "Murder. The killer might not stop with one."

It sounded so dramatic, coming from the cool, practical Isabel, that I almost laughed.

She saw the amusement on my face. "It's not funny, Elena. I, for one, am going to be very careful around here from now on. You should be too."

"Don't worry. I'll be careful."

"It's a serious thing, murder. You should leave it to the police."

"I will. Although I think I have more to fear from the police than from the killer. Lieutenant Kirk really does suspect me."

"Why, do you think?"

"Well, you have to admit that quarrel I had with Frank looks bad. I didn't tell Kirk about it right away because I didn't think it was important. Frank and I quarreled all the time. And now that Kirk's caught on to how much we fought, he's determined to prove I'm the murderer. From the very start, he just wouldn't listen to me."

"About what?"

"Well, first I suggested Frank's killer had hidden in the museum all night."

"Hidden here?"

"Sure. There are plenty of places. Then, when I realized someone *had* left after I did because the alarm lock was set differently when I came back the next morning, Kirk conveniently chose to ignore that. He claims it's impossible because Frank's keys were on the hook when I opened up.'

"Is it impossible?"

"Yes."

Isabel and I stared bleakly at each other. "I wish I'd never bought that *árbol de la vida*," she said.

She looked so woebegone that I patted her hand. "Don't blame yourself. It wasn't the tree that got Frank killed."

"No."

I looked at my watch. "It's almost three. I have to see Kirk in an hour. Why don't I send everybody home now so I can set the alarm for the night? There's no telling how long I'll be." I stood up. "And, Isabel, thank you for listening."

"*De nada*. I only wish I could help."

"You have."

"Good." She stood up, too. "But, Elena, do be careful around here. I worry for you."

"Don't. I'm afraid I'm in more danger at the police station than here."

The police station was only a few blocks away, on Figueroa Street, near the Spanish-style courthouse. On the way, I stopped at the Chamber of Commerce and checked on the current owner of La Galería. Her name, Gloria Sanchez, had a familiar ring. I decided to stop at the gallery after leaving the police station—providing Kirk didn't find a reason to hold me. I bought a sandwich at a hole-in-the-wall stand, then walked over to Figueroa Street. The clock on El Mirador—the courthouse bell tower—said five minutes to four. As I approached the police station, the hunted feeling settled over me once more.

A uniformed officer showed me to Kirk's cubicle on the second floor. The lieutenant was behind his desk, again dressed in brown. His face was its usual blank.

"Come in, Miss Oliverez." He indicated a chair across the desk from him.

I sat, smoothing my skirt over my knees.

Kirk consulted his ever-present legal pad, then said, "Are you still planning to go ahead with your opening?"

"As I told you yesterday afternoon, yes. Except for rearranging the displays in the folk art gallery we're all set."

"Rearranging the displays?" He cocked his head to one side.

"Yes. We're replacing the tree of life with some of Jesus Herrera's *camaleones*."

"*Camaleones?*"

"The Spanish word for chameleon. They're fantasy animals. Jesse claims they change—" Why was I bothering to tell him this? Probably to ward off the inevitable questioning. "Lieutenant, why did you want to see me?"

"More questions, Miss Oliverez. That's what police work is—questions. And legwork. No glamour like you see on TV."

"Well, before you begin, I've discovered a few facts that I think I should pass along to you." I couldn't tell him about the embezzlements, but I could give him the other things I'd found out.

"Very good." He pushed his swivel chair away from the desk and tipped it back. The action annoyed me; it implied he already felt that anything I could tell him was not worth noting down on that damned pad.

"Did you know that Frank De Palma was involved with another woman?" I asked.

"Who?"

"I don't know. But Vic Leary let it slip. He would probably tell you."

"I'll check on it."

"And Jesus Herrera had quarreled with Frank. More seriously than I. He gave Frank a black eye."

"When?"

"A couple of months ago."

"What did they quarrel over?"

"Frank's niece, Maria De La Cruz."

"Oh, yes, the secretary. I'll check on it."

"And then there's Maria."

"What about her?"

"She was sent to live with the De Palmas because . . ." I hesitated. It was unfair to Maria to bring up her promiscuity. "Because she wasn't getting along with her family. Frank was very strict with her. She resented him and seems glad he's dead."

"The way I hear it, there are any number of people who are glad he's dead."

"But his death paves the way for Maria to marry Jesse. She was very defiant this morning."

"I'll check on that, too. Is there anything else?"

He hadn't listened to me this time any more than he had before. "No, there isn't."

"All right." He straightened the chair and picked up a pencil. "I'd like to go over your actions again the afternoon Mr. De Palma died. Start with when you went to his office to ask if he wanted you to set the alarm."

I sighed and began recounting.

As I spoke, Kirk made notes on his pad and nodded. When I was done, he said, "Now, let's talk again about your relationship with Mr. De Palma and the others at the museum. Start with the beginning, when you graduated from UCSB. That was when?"

"Five years ago." I went on telling him about my job interviews, my appointment to the staff, the early days there. Occasionally Kirk would ask a question.

"What about the time you went over Mr. De Palma's head to the board about the Ramirez collection?"

"What about it?"

"Why did you feel it necessary to defy his authority?"

"I wasn't defying. I was questioning his judgment We had the opportunity to acquire a very fine collection of Zapotecan funerary urns, but Frank wanted to put the money into new carpeting."

"Did the board back you up?"

"Yes."

"What was Mr. De Palma's reaction?"

"He was furious."

"I see. Go on with what you were telling me."

And later: "Did you get on with Mr. Leary?"

"Very well. He was like a father to me." The words, in light of my recent discovery, rang false.

"Oh?"

"Vic is very good to all the staff and volunteers."

"Including Mr. De Palma?"

"They were friends. Vic was devoted to Frank. He worried about him constantly. All Frank had to do was sneeze and Vic would be running out for vitamin C tablets."

"Would you say this was unusual devotion?"

"Not really. Vic is a lonely man. He needs someone to care for."

"And you say he was like a father to you."

"Yes."

"Why 'was' and not 'is,' Miss Oliverez?"

But I couldn't tell him that.

"What about Mrs. Cunningham, the woman who started the conflict by presenting that tree of life to the museum?"

"What about her?"

"How do you get along with her?"

"Very well. She's dedicated to the museum. We couldn't get along without her."

"No quarrels of any kind?"

"Lieutenant Kirk, I am not a quarrelsome person." But my voice sounded contentious.

"Did Mrs. Cunningham get along with Frank De Palma?"

"Nobody got along with Frank. Isabel covered better than most of us, I suppose. She's from a privileged old family and was raised in the tradition of machismo, and—"

"Machismo?"

"She was trained to defer to males. Women who are raised like that put on a nice, obedient show, but underneath, they can hate as much as those who weren't raised that way."

"And, I assume, Miss Oliverez, that you were not raised in the tradition of machismo."

"Hardly."

"Why doesn't that surprise me?"

The questions continued. Kirk took a break and sent out for coffee when a patrolman brought him some forms to initial, then continued. More time passed. Soon it was close to seven o'clock. My head ached, and my throat became hoarse. Was he trying to wear me down the way they did on the police shows? If so, I could see how it worked. I felt drained, incapable even of anger.

Finally he slapped his pencil down on the desk and stood. "All right, Miss Oliverez. That's enough for today."

"Can I go now?"

"Yes."

"Good." I stood up and reached for my purse.

Suddenly I thought of something that had been bothering me all during the questioning. I hesitated. Well, didn't I have a right to ask a few questions of my own? "Lieutenant, did you do an autopsy on Frank?"

He looked surprised. "Of course."

"What did he die of?"

A strange expression crossed his face. I could have sworn he was trying not to smile—except that Lieutenant Kirk didn't know how to smile. "Mr. De Palma died of a cerebral hemorrhage. That means he was hit on the head—"

"I know what a cerebral hemorrhage is. Did you find the murder weapon yet?"

"No."

"Was there anything else interesting in the gallery?"

He just looked at me.

"Lieutenant Kirk, I'm acting director of that museum. I think, even though I'm your prime suspect, that I have a right to know what you've found out."

He sighed. "All right, Miss Oliverez. There was nothing 'interesting,' as you put it, at the scene. The only fingerprints belonged to museum staff and volunteers—including yourself. There were ceramic and terra-cotta fragments from the tree itself. Otherwise, we came up with nothing."

"I see."

"Is there anything else you'd like to know?"

"Well . . . are you sure the killer couldn't have hidden in the museum all night? Because I can't figure out how he left otherwise."

"No, Miss Oliverez, that's not possible. All Mr. De Palma's family, friends, and associates have been checked very carefully. Their whereabouts that night are accounted for."

"It could have been someone you didn't check."

"Believe me, we have checked. And you can be sure that Mr. De Palma was not killed by a stranger."

"Why not?"

"In a crime of this sort, which lacks the element of randomness, the killer is usually someone close to the deceased, a family member—or a co-worker."

I didn't like the implication, or the nasty look on his face. And I didn't favor him with a reply.

TEN

LA GALERÍA WAS IN EL PASEO, A PEDESTRIAN SHOPPING arcade in Old Town, not far from the museum. Designed in the Spanish revival architecture popular in the twenties, the arcade incorporates two nineteenth-century adobes similar to the one we occupied. I hurried through a passageway from Anacapa Street, passing without a second glance shops that offered candies, pottery, and leather goods. It was a warm night, the fog spell temporarily broken, and people sat around tables by the fountain in the courtyard, sipping wine and margaritas. From the interior of the café came the sad strains of a Spanish guitar.

This was a tourist area, and most of the shops stayed open until nine or ten at night to accommodate the visitors. I turned away from the central court and went down a second passageway to the art gallery Frank used to own. Although tourists might browse in La Galería, most of its serious customers were collectors with both taste and high incomes. Its front windows displayed contemporary Mexican sculpture on Art Deco pedestals, and inside the place had an air of quiet elegance. Tonight, at almost eight, its showroom was deserted.

I stepped inside and looked around. The walls were hung with abstract art. There were a couple of wonderful watercolors depicting Mexican village life by an artist I had met in Oaxaca; startling primitive-style oils by a local painter; woodcuts portraying revolutionary scenes from a Yucatán craftsman; photographs of migrant workers by one of our more outstanding photographers; and, in one corner, two of Jesse's *camaleones*. The *camaleones* pleased me; Jesse had been having trouble getting La Galería to display them. But there they hung, one a cross between a pig and a camel, the other a startling giraffe with a cat's face and bird's claws.

I went over and stared up at them, fascinated—in spite of this afternoon's anger with Jesse—as ever. What was it about the *camaleones?* Their ability to surprise, often to shock? The fact that, in spite of their grotesqueness, they were appealing? I wanted to take the poor, misbegotten giraffe—or was it a cat?—home and love it. I had the feeling that if it only had a little tender, loving care, it would be all right. Well, wasn't that the way with us all?

A door opened at the rear of the showroom, and a small, slender woman came in. She was in her late thirties, with sleek gray-streaked hair. Her simple black dress and pearls complemented the understated effect of the showroom.

"Can I help you?"

"I was just admiring the . . ." I paused, not wanting to sound too knowledgeable. I didn't know this woman; she did not travel in the usual art circles, and I was certain she didn't know me.

"*Camaleón.*" She supplied the word with a smile. "By one of our most talented local artists."

"What are they supposed to mean?" I made the question sound naive.

She shrugged. "Whatever you wish them to."

I looked up at the *camaleón* once more. "You say he's a local artist. Is that mainly who you represent—Chicanos?"

"No, we try to offer a wide spectrum of Mexican and South American art as well."

"And you buy directly from foreign artists?"

"We have a wide network of buyers, yes." Did I imagine a wariness creeping into her eyes?

"The reason I ask is that I'm interested in ancient art, and I know it's difficult to get one's hands on, given the restrictions a lot of countries have placed on their national treasures."

The woman looked around. Satisfied there was no one else in the gallery, she said, "It is difficult, yes. What did you have in mind?"

I thought back to the boxes I had found in the cellar. "I have a small collection of Aztec figurines. They're inherited, museum quality. I don't doubt I could sell them for a fortune, but there's sentimental value attached."

"I see."

"In order to complete the collection, however, I need the earth goddess Coatlicue. But with these silly restrictions . . ." I spread my hands wide.

"They *are* a problem to the serious collector." Her eyes were calculating. "I could check for you, Miss . . . ?"

"Could you? I'd be so grateful. I'm staying at the Biltmore, but I'm in and out so much. . . . Do you have a card?"

She nodded and went to a small desk. The card she handed me confirmed she was the gallery owner, Gloria Sanchez.

"Ms. Sanchez," I said, "you could be the solution to all my problems. I've been looking—"

"Gloria," a familiar voice called from the rear of the showroom.

Gloria Sanchez turned, a frown of annoyance creasing her brow.

"Gloria," the voice said, "is this all of Frank's stuff?"

The door at the rear opened, and Robert De Palma entered, carrying a red plaid bathrobe. His mouth dropped when he saw me, and he made a frantic effort to stuff the robe underneath the jacket of his tight black suit. He got about a quarter of it hidden, and there the rest of it hung, looking silly.

"Hi, Robert," I said. "Tying up loose ends?"

His eyes bugged out even more.

Gloria Sanchez looked from one of us to the other. "You are acquainted?"

"Sure," I said. "Not well, but we know each other. Roberto and I met in a bar the other night. What was it called—the Bus Stop?" I smiled maliciously.

Robert reddened. The Bus Stop was the worst pickup joint in town.

Gloria Sanchez grinned slyly. "Why, Roberto!"

I crossed the room and took a firm hold on Robert's arm. "As a matter of fact, I owe Roberto a drink. I'll send him back in a while." I steered him out of the gallery.

Robert didn't speak until we were several stores away.

Then he said indignantly, "What are you doing here? And why did you tell her that—about the Bus Stop?"

"Don't act so self-righteous. And take Frank's bathrobe out from under your coat. It looks ridiculous."

"Where are we going?"

"As I said, I'm buying you a drink."

Somewhat mollified, Robert took the bathrobe and stuffed it into the first trash can we passed. I steered him to a table in the courtyard and ordered us both wine.

"So Frank and Gloria had a thing going?" I asked when our drinks had come.

Robert gulped at his wine. "Listen, Elena, Frank's dead. You don't want to ruin his reputation."

"On the other hand, since he's dead, he has nothing to lose."

"But Rosa, and the kids—"

"Relax, Robert. Unless Gloria killed him, it'll never have to come out."

He choked in mid-swallow.

"What was it with Gloria and Frank?" I asked.

Robert looked at me as if I had gone mad. "What do you mean."

"What did they have going?"

"Elena, you've seen her. She's a pretty lady."

"So's Rosa."

He dismissed Rosa with a wave of his hand. "Rosa was Frank's *wife*. Besides, she's gotten kind of lumpy."

Madre de Dios! Was it only my culture that was plagued by men like Robert? Or were they everywhere? A statement like that was enough to make me swear off the creatures for life. "How long had Frank been seeing Gloria?"

"Ever since she bought the gallery. Five years, I guess."

"How often?"

"Two nights a week."

"Did Rosa know?"

"I guess."

"You guess?"

"She knew. But that's the way it is. That's a wife's lot. Rosa had her kids; she never wanted for anything—Frank saw to that."

Hadn't she? I remembered the hard, defiant look in her eyes that morning as she praised her hypocritical husband. She had her kids; she had her pride. But what else?

"Besides," Robert said defensively, "what were you doing snooping around the gallery?"

"Just that, snooping."

"Why?"

"Somebody killed Frank. He had a mistress. Don't the police always tell you to look for the woman?"

"Gloria wouldn't kill him!"

"How do you know?"

"Well, she wouldn't. She couldn't."

"Why couldn't she?"

Robert reddened.

"Why not, Robert?"

"Because I was . . . I was with her that night." A boastful expression fought with his embarrassment.

"All night?"

Boastfulness won out. "Yes, all night."

I didn't know whether to believe him or not. It could be their way of giving each other an alibi. Besides—rotund Robert? Sleek, attractive Gloria? One never knows, does one? At any rate, I couldn't prove it either way.

"You and Frank made a fine pair," I said sourly.

Robert finished his wine and stood up. "I suppose you gave her some story to hide why you really were there."

Belatedly, I realized that the tale I had told Gloria about wanting to buy an Aztec figurine might tip her or Robert off to my knowing about the embezzlements. "No, actually it was the truth."

"Yes?"

"Yes. I'm adding to my personal collection, and I thought she could help me out. But it was a convenient excuse to talk to her."

Robert wasn't too bright, but surely Gloria would see through my story when he told her who I was. Unless she didn't know about the figurine in the museum cellar. How much *did* she know about the artifacts her lover and his cohorts had brought into the country?

I had the feeling things were veering out of my control. I only hoped I could hold them together until tomorrow night, after the opening.

Robert seemed satisfied for now with what I'd said. Mumbling grudging thanks for the wine, he ambled away from the table and back along the passageway toward La Galería. I wondered if he would rescue Frank's bathrobe from the garbage can.

The waitress came by, and I ordered another glass of wine. I was in no hurry to go home to my empty house. Usually I enjoyed the solitude, but tonight it would only be depressing or, worse, frightening. I sat at the table, sipping Chablis and listening to conversations eddy around me. Most of the people were tourists, talking of Mission Santa Barbara, winery tours, and bargains in art goods.

Art goods. I stared moodily at a gallery across the court-yard. It was closed, but its windows shone through the

night. This gallery was more touristy than Gloria
Sanchez's, and its spotlights beamed down on ceramic
trees of life, more tasteful than Isabel's gift, but still
brightly colored.

My mind began replaying my interview with Lieutenant
Kirk: *cerebral hemorrhage . . . fingerprints . . . including
yourself . . . ceramic and terra-cotta.*

I sipped wine, willing the echoes to go away. I was sick
of Kirk, sick of thinking about Frank's murder, sick of
thinking about embezzlement and finding out my friends
and colleagues were not what I had thought they were.
Most of all, I was sick of trying to figure out how the killer
left the museum and reset that alarm. I wanted to forget for
a while. . . .

Ceramic and terra-cotta. . . .

I jumped, almost upsetting the wineglass. Now I knew
what had struck me as odd in the folk art gallery the morning I'd found Frank's body. The little terra-cotta tree of
death had been gone.

The tree of death. *Árbol de la muerta.* An apt name for
what could possibly have been the murder weapon.

Where else could those terra-cotta fragments have come
from? Not from the tree of life; it had been ceramic. The
smaller terra-cotta tree must have been shattered too, or at
least badly damaged, when it crushed Frank's skull. It was
heavy, but not so heavy that a strong person couldn't pick
it up, raise it, and . . . I shuddered at the image.

So where was the tree of death now? The killer must
have taken it away. But what if he hadn't taken it far? It
would have been cumbersome to carry. Where could he
have hidden it?

The museum cellar, with all the other artifacts?

I got up from the table, leaving my wine unfinished, and put a five-dollar bill under the ashtray. Then I rushed down the passageway to where my car was parked on Anacapa Street. I drove the few blocks to the museum and was about to leave the Rabbit at the curb when I realized it would indicate I was inside. Slowly I drove around the rear of the building to the parking lot and pulled up in the shadow of the loading dock.

The most unobtrusive way to enter was through the courtyard off Frank's office. I opened the padlock on the iron gate, then stepped through and snapped it shut again. Quickly I slipped down the path and across the courtyard, skirting the expensive bushes Frank had lovingly planted, and fumbled with the alarm key.

All was dark, quiet. Briefly I thought of Isabel's warning to be careful around here. Nonsense. I had set the alarm at three-fifteen when I sent everybody home and left for my appointment with Kirk. The alarm was still set; I would be safe inside.

Turning on only what lights were necessary to find my way, I hurried through the office wing to the cellar. The flashlight was where I had left it. I moved through the maze of boxes toward the front. A logical place for the killer to hide his weapon would be among the jumble there, where the artifacts purchased with the embezzled funds were piled.

Except that the artifacts weren't there.

I stopped, disbelieving, shining the flashlight on the empty floor space. The stacks of boxes I'd pawed through that afternoon were gone. Faint marks in the dust showed where they had been.

There was a rustling sound behind me.

I stood very still, listening. Silence. Imagination, I thought, kneeling to examine the outlines in the dust.

The rustling began again, closer. It sounded like bare feet moving over the concrete floor.

Quickly I straightened and shone the flashlight back the way I'd come. Nothing. I held my breath. There were almost imperceptible sounds, as if someone else was doing the same. I started around the nearest stack of cartons, to confront whoever was hiding there.

A dark figure rushed at me, knocking the flashlight from my hand. Its upraised arm descended toward my head. . . .

ELEVEN

THE FIRST THING I FELT WAS A PAIN IN MY RIB CAGE. I WAS lying on my side, my head on my outstretched arm. I flopped over onto my back, and the pain dulled a little.

Pain. Now I was aware of my head throbbing, too. I opened my eyes and stared up at a dark, cloudless sky studded with stars.

Stars? I tried to sit up, but the pain was too much. With one hand I groped around and felt a sharp rock and clods of earth. The rock must have been what had hurt my ribs.

I closed my eyes again and breathed in deeply. The air was night-cool and sweet. I breathed once more and identified the scent of young onions. Funny how they smelled so much sweeter growing in the field than they did in the stores. . . .

In the field! Now it all came flooding back—the museum, the cellar, the missing boxes, the dark figure. Who-

ever it was had hit me with something heavy. No wonder
my head ached so. But where was I now?

I opened my eyes and struggled up on my elbows, the
pain in my head making me feel nauseated. On three sides
of me were onion plants. On the other was a steep slope
that looked as if it might rise up to a road. All logic to the
contrary, it seemed that I was lying in an onion patch.

After a moment I sat up all the way and put one hand to
my head. It hurt toward the front, above my forehead. Did
I have a concussion? Wasn't one of the symptoms nausea?
I certainly felt that.

Besides being in an onion patch where was I? There
were farms north of town, but quite a way north, above
Goleta and UCSB. How had I gotten here?

After a couple of minutes my stomach settled down. The
pain in my side was not nearly as severe as when I'd come
to. Probably nothing wrong there but a crimp from lying on
the rock. I looked at the luminous hands of my watch and
saw it was after midnight. I could have been lying here a
long time.

Gradually I hauled myself to my feet. A momentary
wave of dizziness passed over me, but then I was okay. I
looked at the embankment, a seemingly insurmountable
mound of dirt, and then began climbing it on my hands and
knees. It led to the road, all right. And there, not twenty
yards away on the opposite shoulder, sat my VW Rabbit.

What was it doing here?

I stood a minute, catching my breath, then crossed the
highway to the car. My purse lay on the passenger seat and
the keys were in the ignition. At least I had a way to get
back to town. I opened the door and got in.

From here on the shoulder I could pinpoint where I was.

Farmland curved off to the west and in the distance I could see a faint silvery strip of sea. To the east were the softly rounded hills. I had to be at least twenty miles north of town, on the coast highway.

I pushed in the clutch and turned the key. The car spluttered and died. I tried again. No luck. Then I looked at the gas gauge. It was on empty.

Damn! I hated to go to gas stations, always put off filling the tank. Well, finally I'd been caught by that habit—I, and the person who'd driven me here. The question now was how to get back to town. I was in no shape to walk it, but it was almost one in the morning and no cars were in sight. Maybe, though, if I started walking, some late traveler would come along and give me a lift. I picked up my purse, removed the keys from the ignition, and started south down the opposite shoulder.

My head still ached, but not as much as before. The air was cool and fresh, and the sweet onion scent rose up from the fields. In any other circumstances I would have enjoyed it. At least the fog spell we'd been having had broken. The mere thought of being stranded out here in thick fog made me shiver.

As I tottered along, I tried to piece together what might have happened. Someone had gotten into the museum and begun moving the boxes of artifacts, but I'd returned to look for the tree of death before he could complete the job. Who? And how had he gotten in? Well, he'd gotten out and left the alarm system intact before. Given that, I supposed he could get in, too.

I reviewed the events of the night before: I return to the museum before the killer can get off the premises with the stuff. He sees me go to the cellar, suspects I've caught on to the embezzlements. Why else would I be pawing around down there at night? He follows, finds me looking for the boxes he's already moved. Now he knows for sure I've discovered them. He creeps up, hits me on the head, knocks me out.

Then what? He puts me in my own car, drives me north, and runs out of gas. For some reason, he drags me from the car and dumps me in the onion patch. Then he hitches back to town.

Why did he bring me here? Because he didn't want another crime bringing the cops back onto museum premises? Or maybe he thought he'd killed me. I have a slow heartbeat. If the killer was someone who had trouble finding a person's pulse, he might have thought I was dead and decided to get rid of my body. But why? I would have been discovered quickly, lying there beside the road. All I could figure was he'd been headed to a better place, maybe to fake an accident with the car, and had panicked when the car ran out of gas.

After about fifteen minutes, I was beginning to tire. I stopped on the shoulder, looking for a place to sit down and rest. Then I heard the low rumble of a truck in the distance. It was coming from the north and seemed to keep coming for a long time. Then its lights flooded the road as it came around a bend; they washed over me as I waved my hands over my head.

At first I didn't think the truck would stop, but then I heard the hiss of its air brakes as it rolled onto the shoulder ahead of me. It was a shiny aluminum semi. I forgot my aches and pains and ran toward it.

The door of the cab swung open on my side, and a voice

spoke in flat, southwestern twang. "Hey, little lady, the road's no place to be this late at night. Hop on up."

Por Dios, I thought, don't let him be the type who expects exotic payment for a ride. Because, whether he is or not, I badly need the ride.

In the light of the cab I could see a sallow face with a ruff of beard. The trucker was smiling as I reached for the door. Suddenly his expression changed. His mouth hardened, and his eyes narrowed.

"Rough night, lady?" He pulled the door away from my outstretched hand.

"Please, you've got to help me. . . ."

"I don't got to help nobody." He slammed the door. "You're walking trouble, lady, and trouble's what I don't need." He threw the rig in gear and began pulling away. I jumped back to avoid being hit. Gravel sprayed up at me, and I twisted my ankle and fell. I hit the shoulder hard as the truck pulled out onto the road.

I lay there, listening to the truck's gears whine as it vanished down the highway. My headache intensified into waves of pain, and the nausea returned. When I could move I pulled myself to my knees and retched. After a while the nausea faded and I sat back, breathing heavily.

My purse lay a few feet away. I dragged it over to me and fumbled for a tissue. I scrubbed at my hands, then gingerly touched my face. There were cuts on my forehead, probably from rolling down the embankment to the onion patch. I felt through the bag for some hand cream or Chapstick and had a sudden, horrible thought. Frantically I searched the front compartment, where I kept my keys.

The extra set of keys to the museum, the ones I'd

removed from the hook in Frank's office, were gone. The killer had taken them. He wouldn't have to rely on his mysterious method of coming and going anymore. Probably he'd gone back to finish moving the artifacts. Right now he could be. . . .

A second engine noise came from the north—the unhealthy tick-and-purr that characterizes an old Volkswagen. I pulled myself to my feet, half afraid to stick out my thumb. Lights washed over me, and a decrepit black VW pulled onto the shoulder and rattled to a stop. I took a couple of steps toward it and clung to the door handle. It was all I could do to keep from falling.

A round-faced, curly-haired woman stared out at me. "That's a terrible place to hitchhike in the dark! I almost hit you." She pushed the door open.

I sank into the passenger seat. When I turned to her, the woman was looking at me with alarm. "My God, you're hurt! And here I am bawling you out for hitchhiking in the wrong place! Are you okay?"

The sound of a friendly voice nearly reduced me to tears. I had to wait a minute before I could speak. "I feel horrible, but I don't think I'm badly hurt."

"You sure look a fright." She pulled down the visor in front of me, and I stared into a mirror. My face was cut around the forehead, and my blouse was torn.

"No wonder I scared that truck driver," I said.

"Who?"

"A truck driver. He stopped for me, but took off after he got a good look."

"Probably afraid he'd be blamed for it. I should get you to a hospital."

"No!"

She merely looked at me.

"Really, I'm okay." If I went to a hospital, I'd have to explain. They would call the police. At any rate, I would be delayed and . . .

The woman frowned in concern. "You don't look okay."

"But I am." Quickly, I thought. "Listen, my mother lives in Goleta, in the big trailer park near the beach. Can you take me there?"

The woman looked relieved. Obviously my own mother would know what to do with me. "Sure. Just direct me." She didn't ask any more questions as we drove south on the highway and then through the dark streets of Goleta. At the gate of the mobile home park, she wished me luck. I wondered if she'd check the papers later to see if anything about me ever turned up.

I went through the gates and cut across the lawn by the recreation center toward my mother's trailer. All its windows were dark. What else would they be at two-thirty in the morning? I knocked softly; my mother was a light sleeper.

In moments she opened the door, clad in a long nightgown, her hair in a braid that fell over one shoulder. Right behind her was Nick, wrapped in a horrible, paisley bathrobe. I was so glad to see them, I didn't even bother to give them a sly look.

"*Por Dios*, child!" my mother exclaimed. "What has happened to you?"

There's something about coming home to mother that opens the floodgates. I started to cry. She put her arms around me and helped me into the living room. Nick calmly went about turning on the lights. Mama sat me on the couch.

"Look at you!" She touched the cuts on my forehead. "First that awful murder, and now this. I knew I could trust my feelings. Nick, get the first aid kit."

"Mama, I'm okay." I pulled a tissue from my bag and blew my nose. "I have to get to the museum. . . ."

"The museum? At this hour?" She looked amazed. " You are going nowhere with that cut on your head."

"Mama. . . ."

Nick returned with the first aid kit. My mother began rummaging through it.

"What, did Frank's murderer try to kill you, too?" Nick asked.

"I think so."

"You *think*?"

"I didn't see whoever it was. It was dark."

My mother got a wet washcloth and started bathing the cuts. While she applied antiseptic and Band-Aids, I told them what had happened—all of it, even the embezzlements.

"You ought to go to the police right away," Nick said.

"But I can't tell them about the embezzlements, not yet."

"Can't you just say you were in the cellar looking for the *árbol de la muerte*? If you tell them today, they might be able to find out who hit you. Someone must have noticed him trying to get back to town."

"You're right. I'll talk to Lieutenant Kirk. And then, after the opening, I'll tell Carlos and him about the embezzlements." I looked at my watch. "That's only fifteen hours away. But right now I should get to the museum before the murderer takes away all the evidence."

"When did this happen, when he hit you?" Nick asked.

"Around ten."

"It is now a quarter to three. He won't still be at the museum."

He had a point. Time had more or less compressed for me, but I realized it wouldn't have taken the killer that long to remove the artifacts. He'd already taken them out of the cellar by the time I got there. All that remained after he returned from dumping me off was to load them and leave.

"But what if he's left the museum unlocked?" I asked. "And then someone else comes in and steals our collections?"

"Didn't you say he took your keys?"

"Yes."

"And that he somehow managed to lock up after he killed Frank."

"Right."

"This is a very careful killer. I don't think you have to worry."

"Besides," my mother added, "you ought to see a doctor about that bump on your head."

"I'm okay, Mama. No doctors." I hated doctors.

"Just like when you were a little girl." She smoothed my hair back and looked closer at my head. "You could have a concussion."

"But no brain damage."

"Oh, Elena."

"Please, Mama, I just want to go home to my own bed."

"There I draw the line. You'll sleep here where I can watch you. This couch makes out into a bed."

"But—"

"What about your car?" Nick asked.

The car, of course! "I'll have to wait until the gas stations open. . . ."

"I can take care of that. You just give me the keys. The station down the street opens at six. I'll have one of my old fogies drive me up and bring the car back so you'll have it when you wake up."

"That's ridiculous to ask you to go running around at six in the morning!"

"No, it's not," my mother said. "Actually, you'll be delaying him. He and the old fogies jog at five-thirty."

I rolled my eyes. "I think I've been overruled."

"That's right," Nick said. "You listen to your mother."

Meekly I got up so she could open the sofa bed. I got under the covers, feeling strangely like a little girl with the chicken pox. Nick turned off the lights, and they went into the bedroom and shut the door. As I drifted off, I was conscious of their low voices, probably discussing me and the trouble I'd caused over the years. There was something comforting in knowing that certain things never change. . . .

TWELVE

I WOKE UP AROUND EIGHT, MY HEAD STILL ACHING. MY CAR was outside, filled with gas. Mama was making pancakes, but I couldn't eat. She gave me a good hard look and, for once, didn't lecture me about not eating breakfast. She did manage to force some coffee and orange juice down me and seemed to consider that a sort of victory.

As I was brushing my hair before the bathroom mirror she came in and said, "You're going straight to the police, aren't you?"

"Yes."

"Well, you can't go the police station in that blouse."

I looked down. The blouse was torn in several places.

"It is an invitation to rape," my mother added.

I wanted to ask her how she thought I could be raped while surrounded by policemen, but she had left the room.

When she returned she was carrying one of her own blouses. "Just until you can go home and change."

I put it on. It was a couple of sizes too large for me, and the way it fit reminded me of my gym blouse at the Catholic girls' school. All it needed was my last name embroidered on the pocket.

By eight-forty-five I was on my way. Since volunteers and staff would be lined up at the museum, waiting to get in and set up for the opening, I decided I had better stop there first. Certainly whichever one of them had the extra keys wouldn't reveal that by producing them and opening up.

Vic, Maria, Isabel, and three volunteers stood by the front door, looking around anxiously. When I approached, they turned and stared at me and my bandages with varying degrees of surprise. I tried to assess each person's reaction to see if any of them seemed shocked to see me alive. They were all pretty taken aback, however, so I couldn't tell.

"Elena, *qué pasa*?" Maria demanded.

"No questions now. We've got a lot to do today. Do you all know what you're supposed to take care of?"

There were murmurs of affirmation as I turned the key in the alarm switch and opened the carved door.

"Good. I have some things to take care of this morning also, away from the museum, but I'll be back early this afternoon. We'll hold a general meeting at four, to go over final preparations for the party. Isabel, will you be in charge while I'm gone?"

She nodded, anxious eyes on my face.

I took a quick trip through the galleries. Our collections were unharmed. Nick was right; the killer was a careful person and evidently had no interest in anything other than the artifacts he'd removed from the cellar. Reassured, but still reluctant to face Dave Kirk and give him my partial story, I went home to change my clothes.

I gathered up yesterday's mail—bills and a request for money to save the whales—and went to the bedroom. The house had an unlived-in look, with coffee cups piled in the kitchen sink, rust forming from a drip in the old-fashioned tub, and a lumpy, unmade bed. After the opening, I'd have to give the place a thorough cleaning and start spending more time here.

Then I thought, what if the lieutenant remained convinced of my guilt? Could they arrest you on the flimsy kind of evidence he had? Bring you to trial? Convict? I might never get to spend more time at home. I might—

Nonsense, Elena, I thought. When he hears about last night's adventure he'll realize you've been telling the truth all along.

Won't he?

The immediate—and much more solvable—problem was what to wear. I had to go to the police station. Our board chairman, Carlos Bautista, had said he would drop by the museum at one. But I also was going to help with the food preparations; in a small museum no chore was beneath anybody. Deciding on practicality rather than protocol, I put on a pair of faded jeans and a cotton blouse. I went to the bathroom, took a couple of aspirins, and then removed the bandages and looked at my forehead. The cuts were small, really, and without the bandages wouldn't attract much attention. And attention—and questions about what had happened—was exactly what I didn't want. I washed my face, redid my makeup, and then I drove to the police station.

Kirk was in his cubicle, looking as if he hadn't moved since yesterday evening. If he was surprised to see me, he didn't show it.

"Good morning, Miss Oliverez. Have a seat."

I took the chair I'd occupied for all those hours yesterday.

"Have you been in an accident?" He motioned at the cuts on my forehead.

"Not exactly. I'll get into that in a minute. I have some things to tell you."

"Go ahead." He leaned back in his chair, his discounting-the-information pose.

"I found out who Frank De Palma's girl friend was. It's Gloria Sanchez, the woman who bought La Galería from him."

"I see. How did you come by that fact?"

"I went over there to . . ." I couldn't go into that without telling him about the embezzlement. "I was passing by and wandered in because she had a couple of Jesus Herrera's *camaleones* on display. Frank's brother Robert was there collecting Frank's things."

"Things?" He raised an eyebrow.

"His bathrobe, for one."

"How do you know what Mr. De Palma's bathrobe looks like?"

Irritation flashed through me, and I felt it reflected in my eyes. "Robert came out of the living quarters in the back of the gallery holding a bathrobe and asked Gloria Sanchez if that was all of Frank's things." I spoke slowly, trying not to lose my temper. "And, afterward, he confirmed that Gloria and Frank had been having an affair for five years."

Kirk nodded. "All right, Miss Oliverez, I'll check it out."

I was sick of his standard refrain—check it out.

"What else do you have to tell me?" Kirk asked. "I'm beginning to enjoy these little conversations with you."

My hostility bubbled over, and I glared at him. "It all started when I went back to the museum last night to look for the murder weapon."

This time I had succeeded in startling him. "The murder weapon?"

"The tree of death." I explained how it had been missing and my reasons for thinking it had been used to kill Frank.

"And did you find this tree of death?"

"No. Someone found me first." I went on with my story.

Kirk nodded, still looking skeptical, but his eyes were somewhat concerned as he glanced again at my forehead. "You were hit on the head about what time?"

"Maybe ten."

"And came to in this field?"

"After midnight."

"Good. If your story is true, someone may have given your assailant a ride back to town. Or he may have called a cab. I'll check it."

"What do you mean, *if* my story is true?"

"I also want to check your car for fingerprints and other evidence. I assume it's still on the highway where it ran out of gas?"

"No, it's downstairs in the parking lot. A friend of my mother's got some gas and brought it to me. I drove back to town."

Kirk straightened his chair. "Now, that, Miss Oliverez, is one reason for my saying *if* your story is true." He looked at his watch. "It is eleven in the morning. You say you got to your mother's around two-thirty. But you did not call us then to report the attack. Instead, you slept, got up, retrieved your car. By letting another person drive it and then driving it yourself, you probably destroyed any evidence that might have been there. You claim you were assaulted and technically kidnapped, yet you slept, changed your clothes, and, for all I know, ate a hearty breakfast before you bothered to inform us of anything."

I looked down at my hands. He had a point.

"Also, Miss Oliverez, you tell me your assailant took your extra set of keys to the museum. Didn't it occur to you that he might have robbed the place blind? Shouldn't you have called us immediately and asked us to send a squad car there?"

"But he didn't take anything. I checked. . . ." Again, he had a point. It didn't make sense unless I said I knew the person's reason for taking those keys. And I couldn't. . . .

I looked at my watch. The opening was seven hours away. Was it worth keeping silent until then? I could tell Kirk right now, ask him not to do anything until after the opening. But, no, he would probably send men over there, arrest Vic and Tony.

I couldn't do it. I'd worked hard for the museum. For five years I'd struggled to bring it into its own, to give our people and their art the standing they deserved in this community. I was not going to throw that all away by revealing our staff as embezzlers on the day of what should be our greatest triumph.

And, face it, I'd worked hard for *me*. I'd come out of the university with a lot of flimsy theoretical training and landed myself a better job than most graduates. Sure, it had little prestige. Sure, I'd done everything from making coffee to cleaning the rest room. But it was a damned good job for someone whose grandparents had been migrant field workers, and I'd made something of it. If the museum sank in the wake of a scandal, I would sink with it. Then there might not be a second chance for me.

"Well, Miss Oliverez?" Kirk said.

"All right! I didn't handle it well. I've never been involved in anything like this before, and I didn't know what to do."

"Logic should have told you that."

"Then I'm not logical! Would you give me a break?"

"I have given you all the breaks you have coming."

What did that mean? "Look, Lieutenant Kirk, I have a museum to run, an opening to prepare for. Are you going to have someone go over my car or what?"

"I'll have someone go over it right away." He reached for his desk phone. "You can have it back in an hour. I trust that won't cause your opening to be delayed."

I stood up. "I'll be back for it at noon."

Kirk sat, still holding the phone. "Miss Oliverez, I sense you're holding something back."

"Me? No. Of course I'm not. I've tried to help. . . ."

"And that's another odd thing. You certainly have tried to help. The other people connected with the museum merely answered my questions and then stayed out of it. But you've been bringing me these . . . tidbits of information daily. Why?"

"Because I don't think you're doing your job!" The words were out before I could stop them.

Kirk's jaw hardened. There was a measured silence before he spoke. "After your opening, I'll show you how I do my job, Miss Oliverez."

I backed toward the door.

"If your museum weren't important in this town," he added, "and if you didn't have a lot of influential supporters, I'd start doing my job right now—and to hell with your opening." He paused and seemed to make an effort to regain his professional calm. "The truth is, though, I'm rather looking forward to the party."

"You'll be there?"

"I wouldn't miss it for the world."

Por Dios, did he plan to arrest me at the opening? Immediately afterward?

I turned tail and fled.

Now you've done it, Elena, I thought as I ran down the stairs rather than wait for the elevator. You're really in trouble now.

If I couldn't find out who Frank's murderer was by the end of the Cinco de Mayo party, it would probably spell the ruin of my career. To say nothing of my life.

THIRTEEN

I ARRIVED AT THE MUSEUM AT ONE-FIFTEEN, DISGUSTED WITH myself because I had wolfed down a hot fudge sundae with walnuts and cherries for lunch. Its sweetness had not comforted me, only made me slightly sick.

Maria looked up from her typing as I came in. "Don Carlos, to see you." She gestured at Frank's office.

I glanced back there and saw our board chairman seated at the desk. Then I looked back at Maria. "You're looking very good today." Her cheeks were pink, and she had her hair done up on top of her head in a fancy new style.

"I have reason." She held out her left hand. On the third finger was a small emerald-cut diamond.

So she and Jesse were serious about the engagement. I supposed it was in bad taste, coming even before Frank's funeral, but bad taste had ceased to matter very much to me these days. My primary emotion was relief that Maria had something to take her mind off the cuts on my forehead.

"Congratulations," I said. "Have you set a date?"

"We will go to Reno to be married next week, after the *funerario* has been held. There is no point to having a wedding; my aunt would not attend."

"Well, I'm happy for you." The museum would have to buy them a wedding present. I would ask Vic to pick it out; he always chose the right thing. . . . Then I remembered that Vic was an embezzler. He would not be picking out any more gifts.

As if my thoughts had conjured him up, Vic came out of Frank's office, saying something over his shoulder to Carlos. He saw me and smiled, but I avoided his eyes, afraid he would somehow read my mind. I went into the office to find Carlos swiveled around toward the window, staring meditatively at the courtyard.

"Mr. Bautista. Good afternoon."

He turned, a handsome gray-haired man dressed casually in golf clothes. His eyes took in the cuts on my forehead, and he frowned. "Elena, have you had an accident?"

"Only a small one. It's nothing."

"Well, that's a relief." Then he smiled, gesturing at my faded jeans. "At this museum even the acting director does dirty work, eh?"

I took the hand he extended, conscious as I always was of an attraction between us. Carlos was a widower, and I'd sensed for a long time that his interest in me was more than professional. He, on the other hand, must have felt my reluctance to pursue a relationship with a colleague, and had never once dropped his somewhat old-fashioned courtesy.

"I have to help with the guacamole and quesadillas," I said.

"Then I'm sure they'll be delicious." His smile faded, and he motioned toward the courtyard. "Those . . . are those the plants Frank spent hundreds of our dollars on?"

The one closest to the window still sagged to the ground. "Uh, yes."

He shook his head.

"Excuse me a second." I went out and looked around for the stake to tie the plant to. It wasn't anywhere nearby. Finally I located it where it had fallen through the grating that covered the cellar window directly under the office window. The spaces between the bars were too narrow for my hand to fit through, and I quickly gave up. Looking through the window bars at Carlos, I shrugged and went back inside. "I'll find something to tie it to before the party."

"Please. I hate to see thirty dollars dragging its head in the dirt."

I sat down across the desk from Carlos. "What did Vic want to see you about?"

"There are some bills he can't pay, and we've received dunning notices. Fortunately, they're from people I can persuade to hold off for a while."

I felt a surge of anger. The bills couldn't be paid because Tony had been flying first class to South America and bringing back artworks. "What would we do without your help?" I murmured absently. Maybe I *should* tell Carlos about the embezzlement right now. Surely he wouldn't allow it to jeopardize the opening?

"*De nada.*" Carlos waved a hand, his eyes thoughtful. "Vic doesn't look so good, Elena."

"How do you mean?"

"Tired. And I think he's been drinking too much."

"He's taking Frank's death hard."

"That's understandable. They've been friends as long as I've known them, and that's many years."

It occurred to me that Carlos was also on the board of the Hernandez Foundation. "Did you know them back when they worked for the Hernandez Foundation?"

"Oh, yes. In fact, the job that Frank did there impressed me enough that I suggested him as director when we were considering forming this museum."

"I see. Then you must have been pleased that he decided to bring Vic along with him."

Carlos's eyes clouded. "I am very fond of Vic." But he had some reservation.

"So am I. He's a good accountant, I guess, although I have to admit I don't know much about the museum's finances."

"You'll learn. A director must know all aspects."

"Director?"

"You're the logical choice to step into Frank's shoes. I've been very impressed with you, the five years you've been with us. I wouldn't have recommended you as acting director if I weren't seriously considering you to take over."

It gave me a rush of pleasure, until I wondered how willingly Carlos would stand by me if I was arrested for Frank's murder.

I murmured something appreciative and brought the conversation back to Vic. "Well, it will be good to have someone like Vic around to help me learn."

Again Carlos's eyes clouded. "There may be some changes in personnel now that Frank is gone."

"Such as?"

"Obviously Tony. The volunteers do his job for him. And Vic, perhaps."

Did Carlos suspect the embezzlements? His casual, hands-off manner might be designed so he could keep a finger on the pulse of the museum. "Why Vic?"

Carlos shifted in his chair. "Close the door, Elena."

I closed it, then sat down and waited.

"As long as I've known Vic," Carlos began, "he's had certain problems. His ability to get good accounting jobs has been hampered all his life by his homely appearance. Strangely enough, he once was married to a very beautiful woman. She left him shortly before he came to the Hernandez Foundation, and she took their only child, a girl. Vic was heartbroken. He sent child support, more than was required, because he loved the girl, even though he never saw her." Carlos paused, looking as if he wished he didn't have to go on. "After Vic had been with the foundation a couple of years, the child became severely ill. I forget the nature of the illness."

"Kidney disease," I said, remembering my conversation with Vic the other night.

Carlos nodded. "The wife didn't have health insurance. The child wasn't covered on Vic's policy. And the treatment was expensive. Vic scraped together the money for the hospital and doctors, but the child died within months. It was soon after her death that we discovered . . . certain irregularities in the accounts."

"He embezzled the money for the treatment."

"Yes."

"Did he admit to it?"

"Yes." Carlos sighed. "At that point, Frank stepped forward. He said he would make good on the money if we would keep Vic on. He said it would never happen again. After all, it was an exceptional circumstance, and the child was dead. He pleaded with those of us on the board, appealed to our instincts as parents."

"And as a result, you kept Vic on."

"Yes. And, of course, it never did happen again."

"So why dismiss him now?"

"Call it starting with a clean slate. In spite of it never happening again, I've always felt uneasy about Vic. It may seem unfair, but I've always remembered it was Frank who bailed him out. And I've always felt that Frank could convince Vic to do anything he wanted him to."

So Carlos hadn't trusted Frank any more than the rest of us had. And Vic—of course that was why I hadn't been able to fit the big, sad man into my mental picture of the embezzlement scheme. Frank had probably forced him to sign those checks, not through threats of exposure, since his crime had been known, but by playing on the guilt that Vic must harbor. The question now was, how much of that sort of emotional blackmail would it take to push Vic to the point where he might kill?

I looked away from Carlos, out the window, my heart aching for Vic.

"Don't look so gloomy, Elena." Carlos stood up. "It's Cinco de Mayo. We have a party to get ready for." The smile he offered me was tired and cynical.

"Yes, a party." I paused. The party was less than five hours away. My news about the embezzlements would not be all that shocking to him, given his feelings about Frank and Vic. Maybe. . . .

"Señor Bautista?" Maria's voice came through the closed door. "Your office is on the phone."

"Excuse me," Carlos said.

I got up to go.

"No," he added. "I'll take it at Maria's desk. And I'll see you at six." He went out, leaving me alone in Frank's office.

I remembered the sagging plant outside and went to the window. Unlatching it, I pushed the panes outward and looked down at the grate. Maybe I could lower something down there. The curved end of a coat hanger, perhaps. No, the stake would slip out of it. I'd send someone to the store for a new stake instead. Sighing, I closed the window, slamming it, and the old loose latch fell into place. It was then I noticed the crack.

It was a small crack, just a hairline fracture, down at the bottom of the left window panel. It was not really worth repairing. But it hadn't been here when the board members had done their inspection of the premises before we took possession.

I ran a finger over the crack, then went to sit in Frank's swivel chair. I turned it and stared out at the courtyard and the drooping azalea plant.

Once again I swiveled and looked up at the wall. At the now empty hook where Frank's keys had hung: the keys to the alarm system and to the padlock at the end of the court-yard path. The keys that were missing. Those keys and their whereabouts at various times were crucial to the iden-tification of Frank's murderer. I tried to picture them, as I sat there in the chair that, barring disaster, would soon be mine.

I sat there, picturing the murder and how it might have been done. . . .

If these pictures were accurate, they widened the spectrum of possible suspects. The killer had probably . . .

"Elena?" Again Maria stood in the doorway.

"Huh?" I looked up; I might have been seeing her for the first time.

"Elena, it's time to fix the food. Can you come—"

"No." I stood up.

"You said you'd make the guacamole. Nobody makes it like you do."

"Sorry, Maria. I can't do it. Ask Susana if she'll come over. As I remember, hers is pretty good, too."

"But—"

"And, look, I want you to remind everybody about the general meeting at four. I want everybody there—the staff, volunteers, and Jesse and Susana. I want everybody there who is going to help out tonight, so we can go over in detail what we have to do."

Maria frowned at me, disconcerted by my abrupt manner.

"You've got that? Everybody."

"Yes."

"Good. I'll be back at four. We'll meet in the office, around your desk. I'll see you then."

I brushed by her and headed for the exit. I had a little over two hours to get hold of Lieutenant Kirk. And to get his cooperation in setting a trap.

It shouldn't be all that difficult to set one. And I was pretty sure Kirk would cooperate. Once he accepted that I wasn't the killer, he'd be eager to identify and apprehend the guilty party. And he'd have to accept my innocence because I could now tell him how the killer had gotten out of the locked museum.

FOURTEEN

THE SAFEST PLACE TO CALL KIRK FROM WAS MY HOUSE,
where no one could overhear. I drove home, nearly tripped
over a bicycle that one of the neighborhood kids had left
on my front walk, and rushed inside. After I dialed the
police station, I drummed impatiently on the desk with my
fingers as I waited for someone to answer.

Lieutenant Kirk was not in.

Well, where was he?

The desk sergeant said I should leave a message and the
lieutenant would get back to me.

I left one. Urgent, it said.

And then I sat down to think.

A trap was called for, with or without Kirk's cooperation. One that would point to the killer and no one else. I
puzzled for a while, impatiently waiting for the phone to

ring. Perhaps Kirk could come over here and we could plan together. . . .

The phone rang. I snatched it up. It was my mother.

"Oh, good, you're home. Are you all right?"

"Yes, Mama." I glanced at my watch. Two-fifty-five.

"Did you see a doctor about your head?"

"My head's just fine."

"I'm not so sure about that, sometimes."

"What's that supposed to mean?"

She ignored the question. "Elena, you shouldn't take chances."

"Mama—"

"After the opening, then. You'll see the doctor."

"Yes, Mama."

"Promise."

"Yes! Look—"

"What are you wearing to the opening?"

What was I wearing? She was talking about clothes while I was practically being arrested for murder. "I don't know."

"You don't know? It's only the biggest event in the museum's history."

A couple of weeks ago I had bought a fancy native costume. I hadn't been sure about it; the damned thing looked like a wedding dress. But it was hanging in the closet, ready to go. "I do know. Don't worry."

"Do you have a date?"

What next? "Mama, I don't need a date. I can't have one. I'm the acting director, and I wouldn't have time to pay any attention to a date."

"Oh." She paused. "Well, Nick and I will be there."

"Good. Look, Mama, I've got to go."

"I know. You're busy. I'll see you later. And after-ward. . . ."

"Yes—my head." Now it really was pounding again. I hung up and breathed a sigh of relief, half expecting the phone to ring immediately. When it didn't, I sat down in my rocker and planned some more. At this rate, I'd have it all worked out by the time Kirk called.

I got up and went to the shelf where I kept my collection of silver *milagros*. The votive offerings, which are sold at many churches in Mexico, are an expression of our people's relationship to the saints and the miracles they perform. You buy a *milagro* representing the part of the body where a healing has taken place and hang it on a velvet cloth in the church.

The first *milagro* I took down from my shelf was an intricately wrought one I'd bought from an artist who had had a show at the museum last winter. It was a stylistic representation of a woman's head, and I smiled at the irony of that, touching the cuts on my forehead.

Turning, I glanced impatiently at the phone. Where was Kirk anyway? I went over and dialed, leaving a second message. Then I went to get a box for the *milagros*. When each was wrapped in its felt case and tucked into the box, I had nothing to do but wait.

The phone rang again. This time it was my sister Carlota, calling from Minneapolis. She was worried about me, but not so worried that she hadn't waited until the rates went down at five o'clock there. That reassured me.

Without preamble, she said, "Mama tells me you were bashed on the head and the police suspect you of murdering Frank De Palma Is it true, or is she just being dramatic?"

"It's true, but she'd being dramatic as well."

"She wants me to tell you to see a doctor."

I groaned.

"I know. I'm just passing it on. How are you otherwise?"

"Okay."

"Is everything set for the opening?"

"Actually, no. Look, Carlota, can I call you back tomorrow when things are calmer?"

"Sure. Listen, Elena, good luck with the opening. And you take care, okay?"

"Okay. And I will call you." I hung up and went back to my chair. The minutes dragged by. Still no call from Kirk. Well, I didn't need him to put the plan into operation, did I? He'd said he would be at the opening, so I could talk to him then.

I took a quick shower and more aspirin, put on makeup and the white cotton dress. Eyeing myself in the mirror, I decided it didn't really look that much like a wedding dress. And if it did, I didn't have time to do anything about it. I considered putting my hair up, but in the interest of saving time, just fluffed out my curls. I had more important things to worry about than my hairdo.

On the way out, I tried calling Kirk once more, but he still wasn't there, and the desk sergeant sounded clearly annoyed with me. I picked up the box of *milagros*, locked the house, and returned to the museum.

The place was bustling with activity. Red, green, and

white banners—the national colors of Mexico—had been strung across the entryway. Volunteers carried in card tables and folding chairs. A van stood in the parking lot, and two men were unloading instruments. Good, I thought. The mariachi band would be set up on time.

I parked in the far corner of the lot, unlocked the gate to the courtyard, and entered that way. Once inside, I went directly to the cellar and placed the box containing the silver *milagros* behind several other boxes at the rear of one of the shelves. I looked around for the flashlight I'd used the previous times I'd been down here and found it near the foot of the stairs. The scene was set.

Quickly I went upstairs, closed the cellar door, and locked it with the ornate iron key that was always in the latch. I dropped the key in my pocket, looked at my watch, and went into the offices for the meeting.

The outer office was packed. People milled around Maria's desk or sat on the floor. They all wore work clothes and looked hot and tired. I resolved to get the meeting over quickly so they could change and relax before our guests began arriving.

Maria spotted me as soon as I came in. "Oh, a *vestido de boda*!" she exclaimed.

So it *did* look like a wedding dress. "Maria, you've got marriage on the brain."

"Can you blame me?"

"No."

She got up and motioned me toward her chair, but I declined and perched on the edge of the desk instead. I rapped with a letter opener against Maria's coffee cup to get everyone's attention. The crowd quieted.

"From the looks of things," I said, "I assume we're ready to go. I'll make an inspection tour right after this meeting to check details, though."

"And recheck every fifteen minutes until the doors open," Jesse remarked from the back of the room. His tone was friendly and he smiled; obviously he'd forgotten our harsh words of the morning before.

"You guessed it. Right now I want to make sure we all know what to do. Jesse, you and Maria are going to take tickets and pass out the corsages, yes?"

"Right. The corsages are here, in a cool corner of the reform period gallery."

"What on earth are they doing there?"

"The refrigerator's full of food."

"Oh. Okay. Food. Isabel, you and Vic are responsible for getting it onto platters and to the table. And you'll supervise the people who are serving, right?"

"Right."

"Now the important part—drinks. Tony?"

"The ice, it is in the buckets. We have mixed margaritas. The beer, it is in the coolers. And there are oh-so-many cans of soda pop."

"And Susana will help you dispense it?"

"Dispense?"

"Susana will also play bartender?"

"Ah, yes."

"Good. The mariachi band is setting up already. I'll give them instructions about the music. Cleanup crews, please police the galleries regularly. We don't want any of our collections damaged because people are careless with food and drink. Try not to let anyone smoke in there. And keep dirty plates and glasses picked up. It'll make your job much easier afterwards. Did I forget anything?"

There was silence.

"Okay, I want everybody back here by five-thirty. And, even though we're hosting this party, let's enjoy it, too."

There was a murmur, and some people began to get up.

I held up my hand. "Wait." I paused until I had everyone's attention. "There's another matter I should bring up now. I hope it doesn't put a damper on the evening, but it's something you should know."

Their faces became serious.

"I've uncovered some irregularities here at the museum. They have to do with items not belonging to us, which were stored in the cellar. I found them, and they were removed without my permission before I could bring it to the attention of the police." I waited, looking from one face to another. I saw varying degrees of surprise, but nothing more.

"Fortunately for us, whoever removed the items neglected a box of silver *milagros*, which was packed separately from the other things. I've left it down there until the police can take a look. As a precaution, I've locked the cellar door." I took the large iron key from my pocket and held it up. "I thought I should let you know why the cellar is off limits until further notice." Then I turned to Maria. "Can I have the key to your desk?"

"Yes, but—"

"I want to lock this key in there. It's cumbersome. Yours will be easier to put on my key ring."

"Oh." She dug in her purse and gave me a smaller key.

The lock was one of those flimsy ones that could easily be opened with a credit card or nail file. In front of all the witnesses, I locked the cellar key in the desk drawer and pocketed the other one.

"Now," I said, "let's get on with our party."

Everyone began filing out, and I went into my office. I slipped Maria's key on the ring with my others and put the ring in the deep pocket of my dress. Everything was ready now; the trap was set, and I had only to explain it to Kirk when he showed up at the opening. It was time I got on with my duties as acting director.

I turned to see Tony standing in the door. "Elena, may we speak a moment?"

"Sure, Tony." I motioned for him to come in. He slouched into the room and stood, looking uncertain, in the middle of the Peruvian rug.

"Elena, those things in the cellar—why must you show them to the police?"

"Why? Don't you think I should?"

"I did not say that. I do not even know why they are there."

"Don't you, Tony?"

"How could I know? I was not in the cellar."

"Weren't you?"

He rubbed a slender hand over his forehead. "Elena, you are giving me questions for my questions."

"Yes, I am. What exactly is it you want, Tony?"

"I want to know about those things you found in the cellar."

"They're not in the cellar anymore. Someone took them."

"What were they?"

"You know what they were, Tony."

He clenched his fists. "I do not know."

"Tony, the police are going to ask to see your passport."

"My . . . what is my passport having to do with it?"

"It is 'having to do' a great deal. There are stamps in it, all sorts of little colorful stamps with dates on them. They're proof of all those trips to South America."

"Trips?" He tried to look innocent, but only succeeded in looking trapped.

"Trips. You might have been able to cover up buying the airlines tickets—if you people hadn't been so stupid as to use the museum's travel agent and checkbook—but you can't hide the proof in your passport. I guess you might rush home and destroy it and claim it's been lost. But customs, both here and in South America, also keeps records."

Tony's face was ashen.

"You see, I know about it, Tony. All of it. I've only been waiting until after the opening to take it to the board—and the police."

"Elena, why are you doing this? The museum . . . the scandal. . . ."

"The museum will survive the scandal. I'll see to that."

"But where is your loyalty?"

"Loyalty? You talk to me of loyalty? Where was yours when you entered into this scheme?"

"Frank said it would not hurt."

"Frank said a great many untrue things in his lifetime."

"Elena, the dead . . . he is not even buried yet."

"That doesn't change the facts."

"Elena, you must not do this!" He took a step forward, and lifted his arms as if to put his hands on my shoulders. Suddenly I was frightened. In my anger, I had set up a potentially volatile situation. I should never have spoken to Tony at all. He might be the killer. He might take his incriminating passport and run. He might never be apprehended.

I reached up and took his hands, almost recoiling at their touch. They were icy and trembling. "Okay, Tony, calm down."

"But you must not do this!" His voice rose.

"Hush! Don't yell."

"Think, if not of me, of Susana. Think of what will happen to her. Deportation. Disgrace. . . ."

"All right, Tony. I tell you what. We'll talk about it after the party."

A slight gleam of hope came into his eyes. Was it an act?

"You will think again about this? For the good of the museum? And Susana?"

"I'll think about nothing else during the party. But, Tony, you have to do your part."

"My part?"

"You must bartend as planned and say nothing of this to anyone—even Susana. For the good of the museum." I released his hands, and his arms went limp at his sides.

"Elena, you will not regret this."

If this wasn't an act, I felt sorry for Tony—victimized by a greedy young wife who probably withheld her affection if he didn't provide all the pretty things she desired. Used by Frank in his profit-making scheme and at the same time abused and ridiculed in front of others. And now he seemed to believe I would change my mind about revealing the embezzlements because he had pleaded for the sake of Susana.

I began to see the embezzling scheme more clearly. It was like a giant board game, with Frank pushing around the static figures of Vic, Tony, his stupid brother Robert, and his mistress, Gloria. All of them had done as Frank wished, and all of them had been caught.

Well, hadn't Frank been caught, too? Caught in the most final way?

FIFTEEN

EL CINCO DE MAYO. THE DAY OF THE VICTORY OVER THE French at Puebla. Back then in 1862, my forebears had triumphed against overwhelming odds. With luck, I would do the same tonight.

I stood near the arch to the central courtyard, surveying the scene. It was only seven o'clock, but the museum was already jammed. At fifty dollars a head, this crowd would fill our coffers. Funny—a week ago the thought would have excited me. I would have been scheming how to keep Frank's hands off the money long enough for me to acquire some really good landscape paintings, build up our reform period collection. But now, my plan for tonight was much more vital, my freedom probably dependent on its result.

Which one of my friends and colleagues was the killer? Which one of these people—whom, by and large, I liked—

was I going to trap and deliver into the hands of the police? I felt nervous, excited, and a little ill. I wished it was all over.

I glanced at the door, where Maria and Jesse sat at a table, accepting tickets and handing out *corpiños*, red carnations with red, green, and white ribbons. Maria wore her hair swept up on her head, and her lips and fingernails were as bright as the flowers. In between arrivals she would turn to Jesse and whisper behind one hand, her dark eyes flashing. He grew merry, then serious, then merry in turn, and he whispered back. The diamond ring glittered on Maria's finger.

Life had altered radically for Maria and Jesse. No more Tío Taco, no more rotund Robert, no more threats of not exhibiting the *camaleones*. Maria and Jesse stood to have a happy life together—if one of them hadn't killed Frank. I watched them, eyes narrowed, for a moment, then went into the courtyard.

The buffet table had been set up along the left side. Already it was surrounded by gaily dressed people reaching for quesadillas and taquitos, jicama and guacamole. As I approached, Vic emerged from the kitchen, carrying a platter of flour tortillas. Isabel followed, giving instructions on where to set it. She looked haggard, and there was a blossom of orange soda pop on her ruffled peasant blouse; the opening had taken its toll on her.

The spicy smell of the food was turning my already nervous stomach. I changed course and headed for the bar. A drink, a small one, would help.

The bar was even more crowded than the buffet. Behind it stood Tony and his giggly Susana, dispensing margaritas,

Dos Equis beer, and Mexican soda pop. Tony wore a tuxedo, a ruffled shirt, and his lounge-lizard smirk. As the line inched forward, I heard him tell one of our patrons, "The margaritas are oh-so-very strong. They will make it easier to bear looking at the arts."

I stopped moving, and the woman behind me bumped into me. I apologized to her through gritted teeth, my hands aching to seize the Colombian by his scrawny neck and strangle him. Who was he to knock "the arts"? What the devil did he know? Education director, indeed!

I held out my plastic glass, regarding Tony thoughtfully. He looked up, saw it was me, and lowered his eyes. His smirk fell away, and his hand shook as he poured from the margarita pitcher. Some of the sticky substance slopped over onto my fingers.

Tony had never considered me a powerful influence at the museum. Under Frank, I hadn't been. Naturally Tony had never dreamed I would be named acting director, much less discover their embezzling scheme. Following Frank's death he had expected he would be named director and go on collecting an even more comfortable salary, plus be spared the hated trips to South America. And, more important, he would be free of Frank's ridicule and verbal abuse.

I wiped my fingers on a napkin, glared at Susana when she emitted a particularly shrill giggle, and crossed the courtyard to where I'd been standing before. As I sipped the drink, I watched the crowd.

There were men dressed in tuxedos and women in flowing floor-length gowns. Others wore traditional Mexican garb. They ate and drank and chattered, the din rising to obscure the soft Latin rhythms played by the band on the platform in one corner. That would be remedied soon, however; the musicians had instructions to burst into mariachi at eight.

I continued to scan the crowd until I spotted my mother and Nick by the buffet table. She was wearing a bright red peasant dress, and he had on a *charro* outfit, complete to the broad-brimmed hat. They saw me and waved, but my mother's eyes were full of concern, reminding me of the dull ache in my head. I was glad when Nick distracted her with a taquito.

Everyone was here; everyone was having a good time. Everyone, that is, except me. I felt nervous, my palms clammy. Time was passing, and I still hadn't spotted the one person I wanted to see. . . .

I looked around once more, and suddenly there he was. Lieutenant Dave Kirk stood by the bandstand, dressed in his brown business suit, his one concession to gaiety the corsage in his lapel—and that, I suspected, only because Maria had insisted on it when he came through the door. Kirk's eyes met mine, and he raised his can of soda pop in a toast, a cynical, questioning look on his face. So he *had* gotten my messages. I raised my glass in return, relieved.

I took my eyes off the lieutenant and looked around for a place to set the glass. Tony was right about one thing: the margaritas were strong, too strong for the work ahead. One of the volunteers passed, collecting discards on a tray, and I plunked the glass down among the others.

Quickly I reviewed my plan and what I would say to

Dave Kirk. It had to sound well thought out or he wouldn't listen. He'd ridiculed my "tidbits of information," as he called them, all down the line. He had been right about the murderer not hiding in the museum all night, but he'd done nothing that I knew of about the other facts I'd brought him. So far as I was aware, he hadn't even tried to find the tree of death, the murder weapon. Still, he'd have to see the logic of my plan and go along with it.

Marshaling my arguments, I started toward the lieutenant. Before I reached him, however, he disappeared into the galleries. I pushed my way through the crowd after him.

The galleries were not nearly as crowded as the courtyard. Trust our patrons not to stray too far from the food and drink. In the colonial gallery, there was no sign of Kirk, but there was a half-empty plastic glass sitting on top of one of the new display cases. Irritated, I picked it up, wrinkling my nose at the cigarette butt floating among the dregs of the margarita. I supposed I should be thankful that the smoker hadn't put it out on the rug. Carrying the offending glass, I went into the reform period gallery. There, a couple of youngish matrons were discussing the Velasco landscape.

"It doesn't look anything like the Mexico *I* remember."

"What did you ever see of Mexico except the bar in your hotel in Acapulco?"

The first woman laughed. "The ceiling of the bedroom in our suite, my dear."

They started guiltily when they saw me. I smiled and continued my search for Kirk.

He wasn't in the contemporary gallery either. If he was

looking at the collections, it had to be the fastest tour on record. I hurried into the folk art gallery. There a crowd had gathered around the display of *camaleones* that had replaced the tree of life.

" . . . *camaleones?*"

" . . . incredibly grotesque."

" . . . like the morning after."

"Not nearly as grotesque as what happened in this very room the other night."

"This was where—?"

"Right there on the floor, darlings."

"What a way to die."

"Felled by two tons of Day-Glo pottery."

"Well, the fat spic never *did* do anything the usual way."

They all laughed, while I stiffened. The term "spic," even applied to Frank, was ugly.

"Excuse me," I said, pushing past them through the door to the courtyard.

An embarrassed silence fell behind me. Then I could hear the murmur of voices resume, gradually becoming punctuated by defensive laughter. I picked up the plastic glass so hard it cracked.

Why do they come here? I thought angrily. Why don't they stay on their own side of town if they hate us so much? Because it's the chic thing these days. Supporting minority art gives them something to do when they're not sailing or playing tennis.

But maybe it's not really hatred that prompts such remarks, I thought. Maybe it's just carelessness. That, and the tendency—a tendency that's in all of us—to forget that the other person aches and bleeds the same as we do.

This was no time to philosophize, however. Where the devil had Lieutenant Kirk gone? It was already eight o'clock; the band had stepped up its tempo with a boisterous mariachi tune.

Quickly I glanced around the courtyard. Jesse and Maria had been replaced by a couple of volunteers. Vic and Isabel were nowhere in sight, but the buffet table was well stocked. Tony had left Susana alone at the bar, and she was making a mess, pouring margaritas all over everything and everybody. None of my suspects was in sight. The killer might make a move any minute now.

Maybe Kirk was in the office wing. He might have taken a shortcut through the less crowded galleries in order to use the phone. I went over and pushed through the door. Sure enough, there he was, perched on the edge of Maria's desk, talking. I tossed the cracked plastic glass in the wastebasket and waited.

"Got it." He slapped down the receiver and stood. "Oh, yes, Miss Oliverez. You wanted to see me."

"I certainly did. I have a plan. . . ."

"Plan?" he said in a preoccupied way.

"To catch the killer. . . ."

"I'm sure you do, but it will have to wait." He started for the door.

"But it can't wait!"

He turned, irritation plain on his face. "There's been a murder out in Hope Ranch. I have to go up there."

"But I've—"

"Miss Oliverez, I'm a homicide detective. Murders take precedence. You can tell me about your plan when I get back here."

"When will that be?"

"Later." He went out the door.

I slumped dejectedly against Maria's desk. Later. When later? A murder in Hope Ranch, eh? No wonder Kirk had been in a hurry. The prestigious residential area, with its great estates and hunt club, was where many of Santa Barbara's most influential people lived. Of course it would take precedence over anything at the Museum of Mexican Arts.

You're getting paranoid, Elena, I told myself. Of course he had to go out there. It was important that he be on hand right away at a murder scene. And, even though I didn't know Kirk well at all, I suspected he was not at all impressed by wealth or influence—at least not when murder entered the picture.

But what about my plan? I glanced at the desk drawer where I'd locked the cellar key earlier. It was still shut and showed no signs of having been tampered with. Taking out my keys, I went around and unlocked the drawer. The ornate iron key was still inside. The killer hadn't been there yet. I had expected that; everyone had been out where I could see them until minutes ago.

I went into my office, got out my purse, and freshened my lipstick. Things were slowing down now, at least as far as the staff and volunteers were concerned. They could begin to relax and enjoy the party. All of them, that is, except the murderer.

The sound of the office wing door closing alerted me. I stepped back against the wall, into the shadows where no one could see me. I heard footsteps and then a rattling sound. I inched along toward the door. There was the noise of the desk drawer sliding open. I peeked around the door frame.

Jesse stood there, reaching into the drawer.

Jesse! *Por Dios*, not him, of all of them. . . .

Holding my breath, I pulled back. He mustn't see me now. The drawer slid shut again, and then Jesse's footsteps went away, toward the door to the courtyard.

The courtyard! But he was supposed to go to the cellar. . . .

I hurried out of the office wing after him. He was making his way through the crowd of partygoers toward the main entrance. Why was he leaving the museum?

I pushed through the crowd, too, nodding and smiling to people as I tried to keep my eyes on Jesse. When I got to the entrance, he was across the street, getting into his old Chevrolet. In a panic, I ran around the building to the parking lot where I'd left my car. I couldn't lose him now.

Fortunately, my car keys were on the ring in my pocket. I jumped in, ground the starter twice, and finally backed the car from its space. At the parking lot gates, I had to wait for a couple of pedestrians, slow-walking old ladies, to pass. Then I accelerated into the street and to the corner. Jesse had pulled away and was down the block, turning left.

I raced through the stop sign, then slowed down. The old Chevy was easy to spot, and I didn't want him to recognize me rushing up behind him. I followed, obeying the traffic laws, conscious of the fact that I didn't have my driver's license with me.

Jesse drove slowly, too, as if he didn't know where he

was going. He turned left again on State Street and went all the way to where it ended at Cabrillo, the street that ran along the waterfront. There he turned and began driving north, past the beaches and City College and the yacht club. When he reached Shoreline Park, he turned into the nearly deserted parking lot.

I stopped, afraid he'd see me if I turned in, too. The sun was below the horizon, its faint colors still spilling over the blue-gray water. The park itself was wrapped in shadow, its barbecue pits, picnic tables, and play equipment vague shapes under the palm trees. Jesse drove to the front row of parking spaces. His brake lights flashed and then went out. I could see his head silhouetted against the fading light. He seemed to be contemplating the sea.

What was he doing here? If he was the killer, he should be in the cellar, retrieving the *milagros*.

Finally the door of the Chevy opened, and Jesse got out. He stood beside the car for a moment, then crossed to the grass and started walking through the trees. I drove into the parking lot, left my car, and followed. He wandered aimlessly toward the promontory overlooking the Pacific. He sat down on a picnic table. I waited in the shadows.

Jesse sat for about five minutes. The light faded rapidly, and I could barely make him out. Then he got up and went over to a nearby barbecue pit. Seconds later I saw a match flare, and then something flamed up quickly.

What was he burning? Evidence? I came out of the shadows and ran across the grass.

Jesse whirled when he heard me coming. He dropped

the flaming object onto the grill. I tried to grab it, but the fire seared my fingers, and I pulled them back.

"What's going on?" I demanded. "What are you doing here?"

Jesse stared at me, flames highlighting the taut lines of his face. I stared back, breathing hard. Then all at once the tension went out of him, and his eyes became blank with defeat.

He said, "I guess we'd better talk."

SIXTEEN

"WHY DID YOU KILL HIM?" I ASKED.

Jesse looked blankly at me. "You mean Frank? I didn't kill him. I'm not that kind." He sat down on the picnic table again, his shoulders hunching forward.

I sat down next to him, feeling a peculiar mixture of relief and disappointment. Maybe Jesse *wasn't* the killer. But then what had he been doing in Maria's desk? And what had he burned?

We sat side by side, not looking at each other. Finally Jesse said, "You saw me go into Maria's desk, didn't you?"

"Yes. I was in my office."

Again he was silent. Then, "Maria asked me to get something from there. She gave me her extra key."

Of course she would have one. "What did she want?"

"Letters." He reached into his jacket pocket and dropped a bundle of them on my lap. "She'd had them locked up there for safekeeping, but now that you'd taken a key to the desk she felt uneasy. She asked me to get them and destroy them."

"Letters." I looked down at them. They were in plain envelopes without any stamp or address. "Who are they from?"

"Frank."

I turned my head and stared at him in amazement.

The corner of Jesse's mouth twitched, and he looked away. "Yeah. From Frank. Love letters."

First Gloria Sanchez, now Maria. I never would have guessed. So that was why Frank had opposed Jesse's interest in Maria—not because he wanted her for Robert, but because he wanted her for himself. "Have you known about this all along?"

"Not until tonight." His voice had an edge to it, and I knew he was holding back tears.

"How long had it been going on with Frank?"

"It hadn't, not really. Soon after she came to live with his family he began slipping these torrid notes under her bedroom door. She encouraged him, but wouldn't let him touch her. She wanted the letters to continue, you see."

"Why?"

Jesse was silent for a long time.

"Why, Jesse?"

"She was—" His voice broke, and it was a while before he could get it under control. "She was planning to blackmail him. She wanted to get her own apartment, her own car. She figured if she collected enough letters and then threatened to show them to Rosa, he would help her out."

I was silent, feeling sick again.

"You can read the letters," Jesse added. "Read them and see for yourself."

"No." I shook my head and handed them back. "Go ahead and burn them."

He got up and went to the barbecue pit. "That's what she told me to do. They're no good to her anymore. She was going to confront him with them the night he was killed. She seems irritated that she missed her opportunity."

The night he was killed. Maria could have . . . "Jesse, do you think she might have killed him?"

"I don't know what she'd do. I don't know anymore."

"Why would she tell you about this? Why would she admit what she was up to?"

"She doesn't seem to think there was anything wrong with it. She thinks she was clever." Jesse lit one envelope and held it as the flame grew.

"Elena," he said after a moment, "I don't know what to do. How can I marry her now, knowing what she is?"

"I don't know. I don't suppose you can."

His face, in the light of the flames, was weary. He dropped the envelope on the grate and lit another. "The devil of it is, I love her in spite of it."

"How long would that love last?"

He shrugged and added the rest of the letters to the fire.

"Jesse, if you marry her, this knowledge will eat at you your whole life."

"I know."

"Think of your work."

"I know."

"Think of the *camaleones*. How can you create something when your soul is dying?" Unconsciously I had slipped into Spanish; it was not a phrase you could use in English without feeling foolish. Jesse looked at me, nodding.

It was useless to talk, of course. The problem was one only Jesse could work through. I sat there, watching the letters burn, feeling numb.

"Jesse," I said, "when you went into Maria's desk, the key to the cellar was still there."

"Yes."

"Did you relock the desk?"

"Yes."

And the killer would have had plenty of time to act by now. It was almost eleven. While I had been watching Jesse burn some sleazy love letters, the killer had probably sprung the trap unobserved. Dismayed, I got up and headed for the parking lot.

"Elena," Jesse called, "do you know why I came here, to this place?"

I stopped. "No."

"Because this was where we came on our first date. Maria and me. Funny, isn't it?"

I turned, unable to speak, and ran for my car.

The party was winding down when I got back to the museum. Guests were wandering down the walk to their cars, carrying streamers and balloons as souvenirs of the occasion. Inside, a few amiable drunks stood guard over the almost empty margarita pitchers, arguing about the Los Angeles Dodgers. In the middle of the courtyard, I ran into Carlos Bautista. He was handsome in his tuxedo and ruffled shirt, looking as fresh as if the party had just started.

"A splendid evening, Elena," he said, taking my hands in his. "You did a wonderful job."

"I had a lot of help."

Carlos kept holding my hands. Was he going to make the long-expected pass now, of all times? I tried to pull my hands away.

"What's wrong?" He frowned at my abstracted manner.

"I'm just tired."

"Well, tomorrow you can sleep in. The museum will be closed, although I'd like you to attend a board meeting at two."

"Board meeting?"

"Yes. I plan to make your appointment as director official. Perhaps you and I can have a celebratory drink afterwards."

"That would be nice." I freed my hands and began edging away.

"Elena, is everything all right?" An attractive and wealthy man like Carlos probably didn't often have his attentions received in such a lukewarm manner.

"I'm fine, really."

"Good. Also, at the board meeting, I will propose the . . . removals we spoke of earlier."

That would be the time to bring the embezzlements out in the open. "I'll be there."

"Good." He patted my shoulder and started toward the door.

Nodding to the volunteers who were beginning to clear up, I hurried through the door of the office wing. There I found Vic, his face flushed with drink. "Elena, there you are."

"Here I am."

"I've got a phone message for you. That lieutenant. He says he'll be back and wants you to wait for him."

"Probably wants to arrest me."

"Oh, come on."

I shrugged and sat down in Maria's chair.

"Are you all right?"

"Just tired." It was becoming my standard answer.

"Can I do anything?"

Leave me alone. "No, Vic. Why don't you go home?"

"Yeah, I think I will. Too many margaritas. They sure were strong."

I nodded. With a final concerned glance, Vic went out.

Reaching into my pocket, I took out the desk key and went to unlock the drawer, but I stopped when I saw, as I'd feared, that someone had been here before me. The drawer was open about an inch, and when I pulled it out I saw that the cellar key was gone. The killer could have been here at any time since Jesse had removed the letters. I got up and hurried through the offices to the cellar door. It was locked, and the key wasn't there.

That didn't mean much. The killer could have gone down there and searched for the *milagros*, then relocked the door, intending to replace the key in the desk. The trouble was, now I couldn't get down there to check. I had really blown it as far as this trap was concerned. Wait till Dave Kirk heard what I'd done. But then, why tell him? It probably would add fuel to his suspicions of me.

I went through the galleries, checking to see if the volunteers had picked up stray plates and glasses, then went to the courtyard and told them to go. The rest of the cleanup could wait until the morning. I locked up, poured a margarita from the dregs in a pitcher and went back to the offices. I crossed to Frank's and stood in the doorway, drinking and surveying what would soon be mine.

If I wasn't in jail. Could the lieutenant really arrest me on such circumstantial evidence? Should I right now be calling a lawyer? Somehow, I didn't really care.

I went into the office and sat in the padded chair. I drank my margarita and swiveled the chair around slowly, contemplating my new domain. The director's job didn't seem to matter either.

I looked at the telltale crack in the windowpane, then at the empty hook on the wall, and finally at the dirt smudge right above it.

They told the story of Frank's murder, but only part of it. They still didn't tell me who the killer was.

I swiveled the chair back and forth. Windowpane to hook and dirt smudge . . . hook and dirt smudge to windowpane.

Or *did* they tell me who the killer was?

I got up, set my glass on the desk, and began to pace. I would work very carefully this time, making the necessary connections.

I stopped in front of the window, staring out at the sagging azalea plant. I turned, staring at the hook. And then I knew, beyond a doubt, who the killer was. It was so clear, so obvious that I didn't understand why I hadn't seen it before.

In a way, it was a relief. But it left me feeling hollow inside.

I reached for the telephone, to try calling Lieutenant Kirk. I had just dialed the first digit when I heard the noise.

It was not a footstep, as when Jesse had come in. Nor was it the kind of sound Dave Kirk would be likely to make when he came looking for me. This was more of a whisper of motion. Someone was crossing the offices toward the cellar door.

I stood, barely breathing in the darkness. Then I slipped out and tiptoed to the corridor that led to the cellar. Ahead of me, the door to the steps was closing. The key was back in the latch.

So the killer hadn't sprung the trap yet. This was exactly as I'd planned it, except that I'd expected to have Lieutenant Kirk with me. Still, I could wait here and apprehend the person who'd gone down there. Or could I? It wasn't apparent to the killer that anyone was still inside the museum; my appearance would have shock value. Still, I could be overpowered. And then I'd have no real proof. Kirk wouldn't take my word, not against the murderer's.

Damn the lieutenant and his busy schedule!

I stood there in the dark corridor, listening. The walls of the adobe were so thick that voices, even in the next room, were always muted. The floors, however, were merely wood resting on joists. From below I began to hear sounds. The killer, certain everyone else had left, was taking few precautions against noise.

Maybe I could slip down there and watch, then follow to see what the killer did with the *milagros*. I was reasonably graceful and, in my bare feet, wouldn't make any sounds that would be noticed by a person who wasn't listening for them.

Dangerous. Alone, this was very dangerous.

I left my sandals on the floor by the archway and tiptoed to the cellar door. The stone steps were cold on the soles of my feet. I put a hand out to touch the clammy wall, then felt for the edge of teach step with my toes. As I descended, I saw that it was dark at the bottom of the stairs, but the front of the cellar was illuminated by flashlight.

At the foot of the steps I paused. Boxes and crates blocked my way, and all I could see was the light shining around them. Noises, as if someone was rummaging around, came from up there. I inched forward, the cold of the earthen floor numbing my bare feet. The space between the packing cases was narrow, and I had to avoid bumping into them.

The killer had the flashlight, I reminded myself. If I got closer to that light, it would help me confirm my suspicions. But it also could be dangerous if turned on me. I began to feel the boxes around me, noting spaces into which I could duck.

Ahead of me, the rummaging stopped. Quickly I moved behind a packing case. There was a heavy sigh. Then the rummaging resumed. I moved along, one case closer, two cases, three.

"Maldito!" The curse was whispered, the voice unrecognizable. Still, I knew who had uttered it.

I inched along. Another box. Another.

How soon before the murderer found the *milagros*? Turned? Showed me the face I expected?

I reached the last box. The glow of the flash fully illuminated this end of the cellar, but all I could see were the floor joists and the little high window. I would have to step around the box, into the open, to see the killer.

The rummaging stopped again. There was a deep groan of despair. I moved out into the aisle.

And came face to face with Isabel.

Her long hair straggled from its combs. The peasant blouse hung off one shoulder. The upward beam of the flashlight caught and accentuated the lines of strain on her sallow face.

Unfortunately, the beam also illuminated me.

"Madre de Dios!" She drew out the words in a hiss, her eyes widening.

I stepped back.

"What are you doing here?" she demanded. Trust Isabel, when cornered, to try to put her captor on the defensive.

I held my ground. "What's the matter, Isabel? Can't you find the *milagros*?"

"You bitch! You made it all up. There aren't any here."

"Yes, there are." I reached up to the back of the shelf. "You would have found them if you hadn't been so impatient." I opened the box and showed her one, the stylized woman's head.

She stared at it. "That's . . . that's not one of the *milagros* Frank imported. I recognize it. It's yours. I remember the day you bought it from the artist."

"Yes, it's mine."

"Then why is it down here?"

"I planted it. So there would be proof."

"Proof!" She laughed harshly. "Proof of what?"

"That you were the one who attacked me down here last night and removed the other artworks. That you drove me up north in my car and dumped me in the field when you ran out of gas. That you murdered Frank."

"That's absurd."

"Is it? Then what are you doing down here, looking for this?" I shoved the *milagro* under her nose.

She slapped my hand away. "I'm trying to save this museum, you fool. You don't care about that. You would go to the police about Frank's indiscretions. You would bring it all out in the open. You'd drag our name through the mud. All I'm doing is trying to save—"

"You're trying to save yourself."

Isabel's lips drew back in a snarl. She moved forward and slapped my hand again, knocking the *milagro* to the floor. Then she grabbed me by the shoulders and began shaking me. Her fury unleashed a terrible strength.

I wrenched away from her, stumbling back against an empty packing case. It collapsed and I fell to the floor. I struggled to sit up.

Isabel was upon me immediately, grabbing me by the throat. I tried to push her away, but her arms were long enough that I couldn't reach her. I kicked out at her legs; that did me no good either. I tried to pry her fingers loose, but they were locked tight.

Isabel dragged me to my feet. Her hands tightened on my throat. It hurt, and I had trouble getting my breath. I rolled my eyes, looking frantically for a weapon.

Racks of paintings . . . the shattered remains of the *árbol de la vida* . . . a figurine of Quetzalcoatl . . . a bronze and silver Hispanic sword. . . .

My terror brought a sudden burst of strength. I managed to break Isabel's hold on my neck and lunged for the sword. My fingers grabbed its hilt, slipped off. Isabel pulled me back by the shoulder.

I turned, smacking her across the face. She screamed and let go. I grabbed the sword.

As I spun around, its tip nearly caught her in the eye. She stared at it, frozen, then backed off and scurried down the aisle between the boxes, out of the flashlight's beam. Her sandals slapped toward the stairway. I followed dragging the heavy sword.

Isabel ran up the steps and threw open the door. Welcome light poured into the cellar. For a second she stood silhouetted there.

"Help!" she screamed. "She's trying to kill me!" Then she started to run down the hall.

There was a pounding of feet on the floorboards above. They were heavily shod, not sandaled like Isabel's. I bounded up the stairs.

Dave Kirk stood in the middle of the hall. Isabel was midway between him and the cellar door.

"Stop her!" I shouted. "She's the murderer!"

Isabel looked back at me, then flung herself at Kirk. "Please help me! She killed Frank and now she wants to kill me!" She sagged against him, panting.

I stopped. "She's lying. *She's* the one. . . ."

Kirk put his arms around Isabel. His bland brown eyes met mine, shifted to the sword in my hands.

Whom was he going to believe? Isabel, because of her social status and respectability? Or me, because I was telling the truth?

Isabel clung to Kirk, not looking at me. "She wants me dead. Just like she wanted Frank dead. . . ." The words trailed off into a low cry.

Kirk put his hand over Isabel's mouth and, with his other hand, pinned her arms behind her back. She struggled, but he held her firmly.

Relief coursed through me. Kirk had seen through Isabel's dramatics; he'd recognized the truth. Then, looking up at the ceiling light, I realized he'd known even before Isabel had burst into the hall. He must have been here, listening to what was going on in the cellar, because the light had been off when I'd gone down there but had been on when Isabel reached the top of the stairs.

I looked back at him. His eyes, still incredibly bland, again moved from my face to the Hispanic sword.

"So," he said, "who are you supposed to be—Zorro?"

SEVENTEEN

WHEN I GOT HOME FROM THE DOCTOR'S THE NEXT AFTERNOON, my mother was holding court under the pepper tree in my back yard. She had dragged out the blue-flowered tea set I'd bought at a flea market several years before and was serving what I knew had to be Lipton's along with tiny circles of lemon and some very stale vanilla wafers.

I stopped in the back door, smiling. To Mama's right sat Carlos Bautista, looking dignified as he balanced the delicate cup and saucer. To her left was Dave Kirk, looking as though he could use a beer. The two men got to their feet as I went out into the yard.

"What's all this about?" I pulled up the remaining lawn chair and motioned for them to sit.

"Mr. Bautista came by to see if you were all right," Mama said, nodding at the board chairman. "As did Lieutenant Kirk. You *are* all right?"

"Yes, the doctor gave me a clean bill of health."

She sighed with relief and poured me some tea. She'd shown up here early this morning, as soon as she'd heard the news and, after taking one look at the disorder in my house, had started cleaning. She'd been working on the kitchen when I left for the doctor's.

I turned to Dave Kirk. I was no longer angry at him. He had apologized for his earlier treatment of me and, surprisingly, admitted he had not suspected Isabel until he saw her use a key to slip into the museum after the party the night before. Foolishly, she had not thought to reset the alarm once inside, so Kirk had followed, searching through the galleries and offices until he heard the commotion in the cellar.

Now I asked Kirk, "Did Isabel confess yet?"

He shook his head. "It's not likely she will. Her first call was to Al Faxstein, that criminal lawyer. He came right down and has been 'defending her civil rights' ever since," Kirk's mouth twisted in annoyance.

"He won't get her off, will he?"

"No. Don't worry."

"What about the others?"

"Robert De Palma and Vic Leary have been arrested. So has the Sanchez woman, although she's claiming she didn't know anything about the embezzlements. We don't really have anything on her, but she doesn't know that, and we're hoping she'll talk. Some of the funds they appropriated were from federal grants. The guys from Washington are interested in them, too."

"How's Vic doing?"

"He seems relieved, strangely enough."

It probably eased some of his guilt, past and present, to have been caught. "Wait a minute. What about Tony?"

Kirk grinned. Carlos looked amused. My mother scowled. "Tony," Kirk said, "got on a plane to Colombia before we could issue the warrant."

"What's so funny about that?"

"His wife refused to go with him."

"What?"

"She said she would rather make her way alone in the United States than return to what she calls 'that backward place.'"

"To go off and leave poor Susana like that," Mama muttered.

Carlos added, "Don't be surprised if she comes to you for a job, Elena."

"Oh, no!"

"When I spoke with her, that seemed to be her intention."

"She can't *do* anything."

Carlos merely smiled and gave me a very Latin shrug.

We all sipped tea in silence for a time. Then Mama said, "Elena, do you know why Isabel killed Frank?"

"I think so. I'm pretty sure she'd found out about the embezzlements. Isabel was very active in museum affairs. She was everywhere, doing everything from making bank deposits to helping me arrange the exhibits. If anyone could catch on to what they were doing, it was Isabel. And, remember, she was always afraid Frank would do something to ruin the museum. She watched him every minute."

"But to kill him. . . ."

"She didn't plan to, I'm sure. That afternoon, before I left, she said she was going to have a few words with him.

I think she was going to tell him what she'd found out and warn him to quit. Or maybe she didn't even know that much and was just going to question him. Anyway, when I left, she was still in the museum, maybe in the ladies' room or checking on supplies in the kitchen, as she often did. Then she went looking for him and when she finally found him, it was in the folk art gallery."

"And she killed him," Mama said flatly.

"No, I doubt it was that way. She confronted him. They argued. She realized he would destroy the museum, and the museum was all she had, now that her marriage had fallen apart. Remember the conversation we had with Nick? About how a man like Frank would have driven Isabel mad?"

Mama nodded.

"Well, that's what he did. Isabel had always deferred to Don Francisco, as she did to her husband. But, like Douglas Cunningham, Frank finally did something that caused all her repressed rage to boil over. With her husband, she could express it by divorcing him. With Frank. . . ." I stopped. The picture was too vivid in my mind.

"Well, she may not have planned to kill Frank, but what about you?" My mother's eyes were flashing. "She was the one who hit you and left you out in that field to die, wasn't she?"

"I don't think she knew *what* she was doing then. She hit me in a panic. Probably she thought she'd killed me. I have a slow heartbeat, and she might not have been able to find my pulse. The whole thing was pretty clumsy."

"You're too charitable."

"Well, actually if she hadn't done it, I might never have realized she was the murderer."

Carlos leaned forward, looking interested. "Now we're getting to the part I want to hear. How *did* you catch on to her?"

"First, I realized she was the only person I had told about finding those boxes of artifacts in the cellar. At the time, I told her I'd first thought the killer had hidden in the museum all night. That probably gave her the idea to hide there and remove the artifacts after dark. She had to hide because she didn't have any way to get in after I sent everybody home and set the alarm that afternoon. Isabel was the only person who knew I'd found those artifacts and might go to the police. And obviously, she didn't want the police around there any more than necessary. She had some idea she was saving the museum from ruin—as well as saving herself."

Carlos said, "Isn't that a pretty flimsy reason for suspecting her?"

"Alone, yes. But there was also, I guess you'd call it a clue"—I looked at Kirk—"that I'd seen even before I knew Frank had been murdered."

"What?" Mama asked.

"A dirt smudge on Isabel's tennis dress. It wasn't there when I last saw her at the museum, but it was there when I ran into her at the supermarket later that night. It stayed in my mind because Isabel is usually so immaculate."

"What does a dirt smudge have to do with killing Frank?"

"Isabel got it when she was making her mysterious exit from the locked museum—the thing that had us all puzzled."

"Ah, yes," Carlos said. "Exactly how *did* she manage that?"

"This way: There were two sets of keys to the alarm system and the padlock on the gate. The alarm keys had never been duplicated. I had my set, so Frank's keys had to leave with Isabel so she could reset the alarm. But they were still in the museum the next morning. Obviously she had to have put them back somehow."

Carlos frowned. "But if she put them back, she'd have to go inside, and that meant she'd have to turn off the alarm."

"Not really. She didn't go back inside. She left by a door other than the front one; the alarm lock position indicated that. It could have been the loading dock, but then there wouldn't have been any way she could replace the keys. So it had to be the door to Frank's courtyard. She went out there and set the alarm with the key. Then she went down the path to the gate and opened the padlock. She returned to the courtyard and took a stake from one of the new azalea plants, looped the key ring over the tip, and slipped the keys back on the hook on Frank's wall through the bars over the office window."

"But wouldn't you," Carlos said, nodding at Kirk, "have noticed if the window was open the next morning?"

"Yes. It wasn't."

"Then how . . . ?"

"The windows are old," I said, "and the latches work loosely. Isabel probably tested this all before she went outside. If you slam the window, the latch will fall into place. And that's what she did. Then all she had to do was go through the gate and lock the padlock after her. It was as if she'd never been inside."

"But," Carlos said, "how did you *know* this?"

"I put three facts together. First, the stake was missing from the plant nearest the window. It had fallen through the cellar window grate. Isabel was probably nervous and dropped it and then couldn't get it out. The stake hadn't been down there when I left because Frank had just finished tying the plant to it.

"Second, when she slammed the window, she did it too hard and cracked it down in one corner. I knew it was a recent crack because we'd inspected the building for things like that before we took possession.

"And, third, Isabel was clumsy when she slipped the keys on the hook; it's a difficult angle to work from. She got a dirt smudge on the wall right over the hook. It hadn't been there that afternoon before I left."

"And the dirt smudge on the wall matched the one on her tennis dress," my mother said.

"Right."

"My smart daughter."

"Smart? Hah! It took me three days to figure this all out."

"At least you figured it." Mama gave Dave Kirk a stern look.

Kirk had the grace to look embarrassed.

Carlos cleared his throat. "Lieutenant, this super-lawyer—he won't get Isabel off, will he?"

"No," Kirk said, "we've already got plenty of evidence. She had the keys to the museum in her purse when we arrested her, so we know for sure she was the person who hit Elena and drove her up the highway. And we've got a witness, a man who picked Isabel up when she was hitch-hiking back into town. Her fingerprints are superimposed over Frank's on that garden stake—fortunately it's the kind of finish that takes prints well—so we can prove she was the last person to touch it before it went down into that grating. And, finally, we found a fragment of the tree of death in her car—a little terra-cotta skull from one of its branches."

It was a final, chilling touch.

"Well," Carlos said briskly, "we have our work cut out for us. The museum staff has been reduced to two."

"I want to dismiss Maria," I said.

He raised an eyebrow.

"Call it starting with a clean slate."

Carlos smiled; he'd used the same words yesterday. "Do as you see fit."

Kirk set down his teacup and stood. "I'd better get back to the station," he said. Then, surprisingly, he took my hand. "I must apologize again, Elena. I should have paid more attention to your . . . tidbits of information. Ah, can I call on you in the future?"

"For what?" I asked.

He grinned. "More tidbits. Or just some good conversation."

"Of course." I glanced at Carlos and saw a flicker of annoyance cross his face. He stepped forward and took my hand as soon as Kirk let go of it.

"And we must have a conversation about the museum," he said. "Perhaps over dinner tomorrow. I'll call you in the morning." Then he gave Kirk a smug look that made me want to laugh.

Mama led the two men through the house to the front door. I poured more tea and sat there, contemplating the sun through the gnarled branches of the old pepper tree. Mama came back and sat beside me.

"I think they're both interested in you," she said.

"Oh, do you?"

"Yes. I have this feeling, you know."

"You and your feelings!"

"Don't laugh. Didn't I have one the night that Frank—"

"Yes, Mama." I sipped more tea. "Okay, since your feelings are always so accurate, tell me this: Which one of them is going to be the love of my life?"

"Neither of them, Elena. Neither." Then she grinned wickedly. "But they'll both be fun while they last."

Welcome to the Island of Morada—getting there is easy, leaving . . . is murder.

Embark on the ultimate, on-line, fantasy vacation with
MODUS OPERANDI.

Join fellow mystery lovers in the murderously fun MODUS OPERANDI, a unique on-line, multi-player, multi-service, interactive, mystery game launched by The Mysterious Press, Time Warner Electronic Publishing and Simutronics Corporation.

Featuring never-ending foul play by your favorite Mysterious Press authors and editors, MODUS OPERANDI is set on the fictional Caribbean island of Morada. Forget packing, passports and planes, entry to Morada is easy—all you need is a vivid imagination.

Simutronics GameMasters are available in MODUS OPERANDI around the clock, adding new mysteries and puzzles, offering helpful hints, and taking you virtually by the hand through the killer gaming environment as you come in contact with players from on-line services the world over. Mysterious Press writers and editors will also be there to participate in real-time on-line special events or just to throw a few back with you at the pub.

MODUS OPERANDI is available on-line now.

Join the mystery and mayhem on:
- America Online® at keyword MODUS
- GEnie® on page 1615
- PRODIGY® at jumpword MODUS

Or call toll-free for sign-up information:
- America Online® 1 (800) 768-5577
- GEnie® 1 (800) 638-9636, use offer code DAF524
- PRODIGY® 1 (800) PRODIGY

Or take a tour on the Internet at
http://www. pathfinder.com/twep/games/modop.

MODUS OPERANDI—It's to die for.